Ashley & Mocha

MAYA BORDEAUX

Copyright © 2021 Maya Bordeaux

All rights reserved.

Cover Design: Gabriella Regina

ISBN: 9798455696497

DEDICATION

For my love. Here's to many more rainy summers.

CONTENTS

Chapter 1   1

Chapter 2   8

Chapter 3   11

Chapter 4   19

Chapter 5   26

Chapter 6   32

Chapter 7   38

Chapter 8   44

Chapter 9   49

Chapter 10   57

Chapter 11   70

Chapter 12   89

Chapter 13   100

Chapter 14   110

Chapter 15   125

Chapter 16   137

Chapter 17   147

Chapter 18   156

Chapter 19   166

Chapter 20   181

Chapter 21	194
Chapter 22	201
Chapter 23	211
Chapter 24	220

ASHLEY & MOCHA

CHAPTER 1

The neighbor girl was bewitching and had an apparent aversion to shutting her curtains. By night her house was lit up like a big glass dollhouse, and Mocha stole occasional peeks into her various rooms.

The neighbor girl lived behind a MacBook, but she took frequent breaks to shout at her smart home device and scoop up her white cat for a dance around the living room. The cat looked painfully unenthused.

She was striking, with tan skin that would've worked better with the name *Mocha* than Mocha's translucent pale appearance did, and long flowy dark hair. She couldn't see her eyes from this distance, but she had an intense gaze, often trained onto her laptop from behind computer glasses.

One time the neighbor girl caught her looking into the dollhouse of giant windows and smirked at her. Mocha scribbled aggressively in her pink planner to throw off suspicion that she'd been spying.

While home for Thanksgiving break Mocha learned from Mom that the neighbor girl was called Ashley. Mom was mostly focused on how strikingly purple Ashley's front door was. She'd owned the grey house of many windows and purple-front-door for three years but didn't spend much time there until a year and a half ago. She mysteriously disappeared over summers, which could explain why Mocha saw so little of her when she was home from college.

"Your father can't stand them."

"*Them?*"

"They throw big parties. They aren't loud, per se, but they bring over people from Lansing and Grand Rapids to clutter up the street. And for a while they leased the place as an Airbnb all winter, so all kinds of people were in and out."

Mom dropped her voice like she always did when she was about to blurt gossip. "And your father swore she was shacking up with her *female* roommate." Emphasis on the *female*.

Mocha's face heated a little at the backward sentiment, and she glanced at the neighboring house like somehow Ashley might hear.

"Haven't seen the roommate for a while," Mom admitted, turning back to imprinting autumn leaves in the crust of her pie. "They're friendly when I see them at the mailbox. Just odd."

    Ashley's modern house and sleek-casual mode of dress all felt wildly out of place in Harper Port. She looked like she'd been plucked out of Portland or Phoenix and plopped in the middle of Nowheresville Michigan, house and all.
    When Mocha came home for winter break Ashley-the-Neighbor was hosting a glamorous holiday party. The glass dollhouse looked like a scene from a Hallmark movie: cozy, glittering with twinkle lights, and crammed with guests who were a much younger and more put-together demographic than this town was used to seeing.
    Ashley, in a sparkly black dress, roved like the linchpin of the party. She didn't carry herself like a bombshell. She had a reserved manner and savored only one cocktail throughout the evening but she had a mystique and gravity that visibly drew people into her orbit. Mocha tried to distract herself with buying books for her last semester of college, ordering Christmas presents, and scrolling her many wedding boards on Pinterest, but her eyes kept traveling back to that movie-scene party and the twinkling black dress in the middle of it all.
    Mocha had a hawk-like eye for vivid details, for the unique and elegant, for the little things that made life larger-than-life. It was how she brought to life striking weddings for all her clients. The neighbor's sophisticated world behind those big windows felt so far removed from Harper Port as to be another

reality, and it had that magical quality Mocha lived for. It was increasingly hard not to stare.

The crowd behind the giant windows began to dwindle about midnight, but one party guest stayed behind to help Ashley clean up. The two women talked while they put away cups and wrapped up leftovers.

One o'clock in the morning saw them seated together on Ashley's sectional, cradling tiny mugs under the warm glow of the Christmas lights. The party guest scooted closer to Ashley and said something that made her whole calm, composed demeanor change. She stared at the woman for a long time, before saying something.

Mocha wondered if she was about to witness a hookup and finally decided it was time to tug down her blinds. But the neighbor beat her to it. She hopped off the couch and tugged the long living room curtains closed.

Over spring break Mocha discovered that neighbor girl had a motorcycle. She disappeared from the glass house into the garage with a helmet tucked under her arm and whizzed down their otherwise silent street. Dad made a face while tending his treasured early daffodils.

May rolled around and Mocha graduated, sent off her last handful of grad school applications, and settled into town for the summer, ready to focus her whole heart and soul on wedding planning. May was when her path would finally cross with the woman who lived in the glass dollhouse.

Mom threw Mocha a graduation party and invited all her friends from high school, people she'd only shared summertime small talk with over the last four years.

"Did you hear?" Her father bragged to anyone who would listen. "Mocha got into the MBA program at MSU!"

"We have another business major in the family," Mom said, if a little blandly, and dad tugged his arm around Mocha.

"I always knew she had it in her," he grinned. "She's had business sense since middle school and her party planning gigs are taking off like crazy."

She'd worn her red-gold hair down, a rare occasion for her. It worked great to hide her flaming face.

The person she was around her clients all but disappeared around her parents.

What Dad didn't know was that, while a Master's degree had always been a part of her dream, she had no plans to go into business for one of his stiff connections or sister companies. When she'd heard how practical the MBA at Michigan State was, that she could focus on entrepreneurship, and that she got to develop her own business model throughout, she'd been sold. The pond at her little religious college had been small, but the connections she'd make at MSU would be invaluable.

And since Dad would be paying for her MBA, she wouldn't tell him that this "wedding planning gig" was what she planned on doing for the rest of her life, or that she wanted to someday employ other wedding planners, and have a whole list of vendor partners, and build a premier one-stop-shop wedding service. He would laugh like she was a middle schooler trying to go big with a lemonade stand.

She was still charging on the lower end, still getting her name out, still making vendor connections. But with each wedding, her confidence and passion grew. Bringing visions to life was her thing and she didn't have any plans to stop.

"So will you be living here?" Blake Kelvin asked. She couldn't believe Mom had invited Blake Kelvin.

"I will," she said a little hesitantly, but added quickly, "At least for the first semester!" She was looking forward to the half-hour commute. The short drive between Harper Port and undergrad hadn't made her feel far enough away, but she'd found roommates after the first semester, and maybe she'd get that lucky again.

The party ended and Mocha fled to the mailbox.

Purging her closet was how she'd kicked off each summer, and this year her ancient collection of underwear was the first thing to go. The risk of her parents opening her mail was never zero and she wanted to get to the panty packages before her mom could. Cute new underwear would be a welcome consolation prize for that uncomfortable party.

She cradled the parcel beneath her arm as she darted up the steps.

"Oooh, who is that from?" Mom called, dusting the mantle.

"A friend from school I think!" She called, not

pausing her flight up the stairs.

Once safely in her room she plucked up her pink scissors and neatly sliced into the package. She pushed past the paper… and tugged out strappy, complicated black panties that looked like they belonged to a bondage set.

CHAPTER 2

Ashley's phone buzzed with a text from her sister. *Tess's sapling is growing like crazy!*

Included was a picture of what was finally starting to look like a little tree, the beginnings of a red maple. In the background, not too far down the path, Grandma's oak was looking more established. Both were unfurling in the tranquil May sunshine.

Ashley knew her sister meant the text to be hopeful and happy but she felt her throat close and the world tilt. Then the strangest feeling followed that flood of ache.

Relief.

She was relieved she still had the capacity to feel broken.

The world wasn't ripped apart anymore when she heard Tessa's name. The pangs of heartache were fewer and farther in between. Guilt followed the realization that in some small secret core part of her, she wanted to get on with her life.

It made her feel sick.

It's stunning. Thank you, Riley.

She sipped her second espresso of the day and distracted herself by opening mail. She jaggedly sliced into a package with a pocketknife. She used to change her hair whenever she felt sad or like she wanted some semblance of control in her life, but these days she just bought new underwear. Maybe it was expressly because no one would even see it. It was purely and simply to make herself feel good, a defiant and sexy self-care. She'd moved past anything to do with how people perceived her.

She ripped out the tissue paper and tugged out the contents… and three dainty bra-and-panty sets came spilling out. One pink, one lilac, one teal, none of them like anything she would wear, and definitely none that would fit.

She wrinkled her nose and checked the label.

Shit, it must be for the girl next door, the one who spied on her sometimes like she was watching a witch conducting seances. She had that wholesome Duggar daughter vibe for days.

She peered over at the neighbor's house to see if she could spy anything. A lamp was lit in the upper room, and it looked like Duggar girl was up there, sitting at her desk by the window.

And in a stroke of luck, she noticed Ashley, peering at her from her own upper office.

She lifted the handful of underwear in a questioning gesture.

In response, the girl rifled through something on her floor and sheepishly lifted a handful of underwear, all black.

Ashley smirked and proffered a thumbs-up. Then she pointed out front towards the mailboxes.

The neighbor girl nodded. She was strikingly pretty, Ashley realized. Stunning, if she was honest. If she didn't look so meek she'd have vintage Hollywood golden-girl looks.

Ashley crammed the frilly underwear into its package and carried the parcel out to the mailbox. She didn't particularly feel like small talk, so pushed the package into the appropriate box, slammed it shut, and headed back inside. A little bit later when the girl crept out to collect her package and shove Ashley's into its box, Ashley waved politely from the window.

The girl blushed a little when she waved back.

CHAPTER 3

Mocha's website was starting to look like the real deal, her portfolio sporting over two dozen weddings. This summer was her chance to get into a real wedding vendor swing with weddings every weekend and couple meetings all week long. She finished uploading pictures of the wedding she'd organized last month and a glowing testimonial from the bride.

It had surprised everyone at school that the occasional bridezilla couldn't shake her love of weddings. No matter how demanding the personality she managed to pull things together, and it was even more rewarding when the most demanding brides came away with dreamy satisfaction.

She was meeting with a couple this afternoon and her cousin's engagement party was this evening. She'd helped her aunt organize the event from a distance.

Cousin Cora's wedding was the event of the season, and she had been quick to snap up Mocha to plan every single pre-wedding event because *"My maid of honor is more so in name only. She won't do shit."* So Mocha was the real force behind the engagement party, *both* of Cora's bridal showers, the bachelorette party, and the wedding weekend events.

The pressure was on. She knew the family pretty much thought she planned backyard birthday parties, and that all judgmental eyes would be on her as she strung together Cora's glamorous estate wedding.

She thrived on the challenge.

She put the finishing touches on her website updates, felt a small swell of pride at the crisp and polished layout she'd put together herself, and shut her laptop.

Mom was freaking vacuuming again, feverishly, and Dad was walking around the house in a suit, home for lunch.

"Where are you heading Mocha?" he asked, swigging his health shake, the texture of scummy pond water. Mom mixed that sewer sludge up for him every single day of her life and she did it with a winning smile.

Sometimes Mom gave Mocha a weird look these days. Mom had never gone to college, and she always said with a small crack in her voice that, *"I always wanted to be a housewife and stay-at-home-mother."* Sometimes Mocha wondered whether it was envy she saw in Mom's recent eerie stare.

She kept the business-running and master's-degree-earning talk to a minimum around Mom.

"Don't forget your cousin's party tonight!" Mom called.

"Of *course* not, Mom!" Mocha refrained from blurting that she'd planned the whole thing.

It wasn't hard to abide by their-house-their rules. Mocha had always found being good... easy. She'd been a good girl in school, at church, in Girl Scouts, and in 4-H, but she wasn't that sniveling trying-too-hard good girl. It all came authentically. Naturally.

She liked orderliness and she liked getting things done. And her parent's overbearingness was a small price to pay for free education and free housing.

That night her aunt and uncle's towering blue home was a twinkling wonderland with lights that she'd put up, a dorky photo booth with hats and props, and a whole spread of kebobs, groom's request.

"Mochi!" Cousin Cora called out her family nickname and tugged her into a fierce perfume-smelling hug. "It's all so pretty! I can't believe it's happening. I can't believe I'm getting married!"

"It'll be a fairytale," Mocha promised. "You've got such a good guy." She waved at Mason, the groom, who was already devouring a kebob. "I'm relieved too. You sure dated a lot of jerks before Mason."

"Hey, I needed to get the douchery out of my system before I was ready to settle." She grinned at Mason, and then past him. "Oh look, the photographer is here! You're going to love her. I'll hook you up so you can talk about wedding-ey things."

She'd hired the photographer before hiring Mocha. She'd been hired to photograph every single pre-wedding event, Aunt Elsie's orders. Mocha silently prayed this photographer would be professional. She hadn't had the best of luck with them, and way too many brides asked friends and family members to photograph, and then cried their eyes out when their photos came out as amateurish as you'd expect from a cousin who also happens to own a camera.

She'd worked with a lot of photography majors who really should stick to landscape photography because they didn't know how to talk to or shoot people, angsty hipsters who didn't know you could edit in anything other than sepia, and endless film majors who did this "as a side gig" but felt it was a waste of their talents.

So, photographers were painfully lacking in her list of contacts to suggest to brides. She could help them pick literally anybody else, from DJs to caterers and cake artists, but when it came to photographers, 'For the love of God, not your cousin-who-doesn't-actually-know-how-to-work-their-camera,' was the best recommendation she could muster.

She went to the front door and almost plowed into her next-door neighbor, in the flesh, outside of the glass dollhouse.

"Ashley!" she blurted, before remembering that they'd never actually met in person before, so it was probably cringey that she knew her name. The woman raised a slight eyebrow and Mocha fumbled to quickly recover. "Ashley is your name, isn't it? I think you're my neighbor."

She saw a camera bag slung over her shoulder.

Photo editing. That's what she was always doing on her MacBook then, day and night. And that was why she disappeared on the weekends and in the summertime— she was out photographing weddings. Now that she was close enough she could finally see that her eyes were hazel brown.

"So you've already met!" Cora grinned.

"Not exactly," Mocha admitted.

"Well, Ashley Montez, this is my cousin, up-and-coming wedding planner Mocha Johnson. Mocha, officially meet Ashley. I booked her the instant I knew I was getting married."

They shook hands and Mocha chalked the little buzz she felt up to dim embarrassment.

"Her shit's amazing," Cora said. "I knew there was no way I was gonna have just anybody take our photos!"

"Good call," Mocha grinned. Luckily, when she was in planner mode, she was in her element, so she was able to dial it back and put on composure pretty quickly. "I'm sure we'll talk more later! Nice to meet you, Ashley."

Ashley nodded and went to take pictures of the details and cutesy kebob signage and decor before Mason could eat the whole table.

The party went off without a hitch.

Wine, beer and cheese bar, kebobs, how-well-do-you-know-the-couple games, and one grinning couple all stitched together into the perfect evening. Everyone told her aunt and uncle they'd planned such a beautiful affair, and that was all the affirmation Mocha needed.

As the evening began to wind down she stepped outside to check on how the fire pits and s'mores stations were faring.

Ashley was snapping candid photos of Cora and Mason engaged in hushed conversation on the porch swing, and the other couples hovering by the property pond.

Since the evening was almost over, Mocha approached Ashley. Ashley didn't turn to face her, or waste time with greetings, just continuing to capture the activity and people milling on the lush landscape.

"I think a few of my brides booked you to coordinate when they heard you were back in town. Bea Evans and Claire Morris?"

"Yes!" Mocha said, surprised. It only just now clicked that she totally knew each had hired an *Ashley Montez* as their photographer. This Ashley Montez, of course.

Ashley turned to face her; Mocha assumed to talk—but she snapped a photo of her instead.

She hadn't been prepared for it and didn't know which expression to put on her face in response.

"Your name is unique," Ashley said, unscrewing her lens to put on a different one.

People asked stupidly often if it was a family name and she always felt obligated to launch awkwardly into the story. "Mom craved white chocolate mochas when she was pregnant with me and she thought 'Mocha' was cute and she couldn't get it out of her head. Dad said he'd go along with it only if my middle name was May after my grandma. He hoped everybody would call me May, but Mocha stuck."

"It's cute. And at least she didn't try to name you White Chocolate Mocha."

"You're right." Mocha wasn't very good at banter with people she didn't know.

Ashley looked through her lens and then lowered the camera. "Cora's mom is having me capture absolutely everything from the yes-to-the-dress to the bridal shower and the bachelorette. Everything. I'm not complaining, but you'll probably get sick of me this summer."

"Aune Elsie likes to document," she said, apologetically. "And Cora doesn't mind a good Instagram spam either. Wanna set up a few meetings so we can talk through all of Cora's events? And each bride's vision?"

Ashley's low little smile was more bewitching than Mocha wanted to admit to herself.

"I'm pretty sure you live right next door to me. Wanna come over tomorrow?"

That night Mocha stalked Ashley Montez's

website.

"Oh my gosh!"

Holy professional freaking bliss.

Ashley's page was sleek and elegant, her portfolio bursting at the seams.

The photo editing seemed tailored to each bride's vision, bright and colorful, or moody and twinkle-lit, or luxury and black-and-white.

But it was all shot in a distinctive style, which felt cinematic but candid and authentic. Like she'd just happened to stumble onto and photograph a fairytale.

Mocha was instantly in love. With the work, of course.

Mocha, you might have a slight stalking problem, she internally chided herself, scrolling through the inspiration-rich weddings late into the night. She'd finally found a photographer she could recommend.

CHAPTER 4

Ashley watched Mocha pick her way down the pathway like she was creeping up to a haunted house. Blossom petals fell around her in the breeze, and she'd make a striking portrait if she didn't look a little like a frightened sheep cradling a giant tote bag. The poised woman she'd been while blitzing around to run the engagement party didn't seem to be her default. She knew plenty of wedding vendors who were the same way—DJs who were only fun on the dance floor, cake artists who couldn't stand sugar. It was a little hard for Ashley to get her head around. She'd never learned how to un-synthesize the parts of herself.

She swigged her espresso in preparation for the visit. The neighbor girl was adorable. Also, she got the feeling she had never been alone in a room with a lesbian person-of-color in her life. The backward-church-girl-vibe was strong with that one, and Ashley wondered if she baked pies or played hymns on the harp to entice her lovers.

She told herself to give the girl a chance and went to get the door before Mocha could knock.

"Hey. Come in." She flung the purple door open wider for Mocha to step inside and headed into the living room.

Mocha looked around her in wonder. Ashley knew full well not many houses in this part of Michigan looked anything like modern inside. The black and white fixtures, pops of mahogany, and black marble countertops were her pride and joy. The gigantic windows, however, were the highlight of her life, and she couldn't stand to keep them curtained.

Mocha stopped in front of a wall of pictures arranged around a tapestry Tess had bought in Peru. The pictures were of their travels. Morocco. Spain. Mayan ruins in Belize. Horseback riding in Costa Rica.

As if it were entirely involuntarily, Mocha blurted, "Why the heck do you live out here?" Then she immediately looked like she wished she could take it back.

Ashley laughed at the surprising blurt. "Well. It's a half-hour to Lansing, an hour and a half to Grand Rapids, under two hours to Lake Michigan and Erie both. Way affordable property." She plopped down at her desk, the window beside it open to let in the grassy and blossom-ey air, which was starting to warm with a hint of summer. "And my girlfriend always wanted to live in a cozy, tiny town."

She wondered if that was faint disappointment she saw on Mocha's face at the mention of a *girlfriend*. "How do you like it?"

"Mmm," She pulled on her computer glasses, opened her laptop, and started pulling up the Evernote notebooks she made for each bride. "At first people gave us all kinds of looks. Some were outright hostile. I asked her why we didn't just leave, go to the coast, Saugatuck, or something. She gave me this diabolical little look and said, 'No, I think we'll stay.' And that was that."

"How long have you two been together?" she asked politely.

"We were together since we were sixteen."

Mocha blinked rapidly, no doubt bewildered by someone who would keep this many photos of their ex on the wall.

She didn't like people speculating so she cut to the chase.

"She died." She swigged the last sip from her little espresso mug.

"I am so sorry!"

She knew the next question people really wanted to ask was *what happened?* So she got that out of the way too.

"Autoimmune disease she didn't know she had. I came home from work one day. I thought she was sleeping." Her eyes flicked to the view from the window. "She had passed."

Mocha looked completely stricken. "I am so incredibly sorry!"

"I miss her. But we had a good life together. Coffee?"

"Um," Mocha's green gaze was glassy like she'd been about to cry, and she took a second to pull herself together. "Do you have any tea by chance?"

"It's all really old." Tess had liked the occasional cup of tea.

"That's okay, I'll just take two teabags."

If it had been literally anybody else she'd have teased them for their word choice, but she really didn't know how Mocha would handle that, particularly after just talking about premature death.

So she let the moment pass and opened the coffee cupboard for her to look through the few boxes of tea. She picked chamomile.

"It's a really lovely house," She called, peering out the patio door while the kettle started bubbling to life.

"I'm thinking of renting or selling and moving back to Wisconsin."

"Back to Wisconsin?"

She'd had enough deep dark conversation for one day, so glossed over that lifetime. "I have a large client base here, but I do a lot of work in Wisconsin too."

Clearly unsure what to do with herself, Mocha drifted again, this time to look at a panel of pictures in the kitchen.

"My favorite places," Ashley explained absently, plopping two teabags into a blue mug that had been Tess's favorite. "My grandmother's house. And North Point Lighthouse."

She poured the steaming water over the chamomile

bags and came to stand beside Mocha, who was still staring up at the photos.

One was of Ashley, her sister, and her mom, all huddled together in front of the North Point Lighthouse with its white walls and red roofing. Her Hispanic ancestry was most visible in her mother, and the Cherokee most visible in her sister. Ashley fell somewhere between them, features reflecting both.

The other photo was of her and Tess, sixteen, with scarlet hair and dark hair running wild, sitting on her grandma's porch steps. She hadn't looked closely at it in a long time.

"Bridal visions?" She prompted, handing Mocha the cup of tea. "You were here to discuss bridal visions?"

"Oh. Yeah."

She took a seat and rifled through her tote bag, producing an organizer, a folder, a spiral notebook, and a tablet that opened immediately to Pinterest boards.

Ashley tugged out the single white legal pad in which she scribbled everything before typing it up.

Mocha really was striking, even more so up close, and charming when she relaxed. Her passion and drive were palpable.

"Claire Morris is going for vintage. Think sepia." She said it with slight disdain.

"Not a sepia kind of girl?" Ashley laughed.

"It's a pet peeve," she looked a little abashed, like she hadn't meant for Ashley to catch that tiniest hint of revulsion. "I guess because I too can take a grainy photograph and turn it brown with an app on my phone."

Ashley laughed and wrote down *sepia*.

Mocha cleared her throat and went on. "Bea's really going for a romantic feel and wants her photos to reflect that. Dreamy and kinda..."

"Moody."

"Yeah!" It took a beat for her to realize Ashley was being sarcastic. "Dreamy," she repeated firmly. "Think dim lights and *Phantom of the Opera* tones."

She'd never heard 'Phantom of the Opera tones' used in a sentence before.

"So, the opposite of your cousin."

"Yes." She grinned. "Cora's wedding has to look like a Taylor Swift music video. Pastel and romantic and light and airy and like magic."

"So if you were a wedding," Ashley almost said, but refrained.

"Magic. Got it."

This discussion went on for a good hour, but it didn't feel like it. She did a double-take when she saw the time.

"And your cousin's going for two ageist segregated bridal showers, right?"

Mocha looked astonished.

"One for friends and young cousins and then one for aunts, grandmas, and old church ladies, right?"

"Yes." She cleared her throat. "One put on by her maid of honor and one put on by her church. Different invite list."

When everything was wrapped, Ashley walked her

to the door and Mocha turned back stiffly. "So, I'll see you at the bridal shower next week?"

"Wouldn't miss it for the world."

She looked like she wished to engage with the deadpan banter but didn't quite know how to. She nodded, smiled weakly, and shuffled home.

CHAPTER 5

Cora was already mimosa-drunk when she seized Mocha's arm. "Look. There's this *thing.*"

"I'll take care of it," she said quickly, not even waiting to hear what *it* was.

"My friend Beth has no filter. And she definitely caught me and Mason doing it once. Mom of course—"

"Thinks you're still a virgin."

"*Rightt.* Just don't let her anywhere near my mom or sisters, okay?"

"Of course," she grinned.

Then she thought she noticed Ashley over by the mimosa bar but couldn't be sure from behind.

"And you know how Mom and cousin Debbie go at it with politics." Which was funny, because when it came down to it they were really similar politically. "If you could just do what you can to kind of keep them away from each other?"

"Of course," she said, with a tiny pinprick more distraction this time.

Ashley turned just as Mocha was sipping from her glass—and she swallowed wrong.

Ashley was wearing a lace, light purple dress with long sleeves that outlined her every curve with a sexy, sweet effortlessness. She wore it like she was unaware of it, like she was wearing an oversized t-shirt and leggings, and to anyone else, she might have blended into the background while she photographed the mimosa bar, frilly little quiches and cakes, faux diamond rings, and cupcakes with lingerie fondant.

Mocha told herself the buzz was just mimosa.

Ashley saw her and waved.

She waved stupidly back and tried to play it cool when Ashley approached.

"I overheard the bachelorette party plans got changed?"

"Oh, yeah, it's become a bachelorette weekend."

"I might need the details on that. I'm supposed to be there."

A rush of boldness welled in Mocha out of nowhere, probably due in part to the champagne with a spritz of orange juice. "Maybe we could grab coffee after this?"

Ashley nodded, unaffected. "I can show you the engagement party photos before I send them back to the bride."

"And then I can see if you're up for a Mackinac

wedding I was just asked to plan? They haven't hired a photographer yet."

Mocha's insides fluttered again at Ashley's little smile. "I love Mackinac. Sounds good."

She stepped away to photograph sparkling glasses of Moscato that a cousin had piled onto a tray. Then they drifted apart, Mocha to recover from these strange tingles and see that everything ran smoothly, Ashley to capture every antic.

Everyone had brought lingerie and cooking utensils for the bride, like panties and rolling pins were a logical pairing. The mimosa and Moscato toasts were endless. The games were appropriately corny and elicited the expected snickers.

And all in all, it was a beautiful success, Beth didn't spill any sexual secrets to anyone, Aunt Elsie and Debbie hardly crossed paths and had no time to argue over which candidate could accomplish exactly the same thing but better, and Cora was smiling at the end.

Ashley was arranging some loose lingerie against a backdrop of glasses, champagne bottles, and signage for a picture when Mocha found her again.

"I'm gonna help clean up. Meet you in like an hour and a half? Do you like The Flower Box?"

Ashley agreed and the appointment was set.

Mocha gathered up the lingerie for Cora, gathered up the remnants of each game, made short work of bottles and glasses, and then worked around the few remaining friends and cousins to take down signs and frills.

Cora finally shooed her few remaining guests out the door and helped Mocha scoop cupcake remnants into bins with one hand while cradling a glass of wine with the other.

"So," Mocha asked casually. "Is the photographer shooting the second bridal shower too?"

"Oh shoot. Mom *did* ask her to photograph every pre-wedding event, didn't she? I didn't even think about it. The church'll probably burst into flames if Ashley walks inside."

Mocha stared at her cousin in surprise. Cora had gone to public school and MSU after that and was the last one she'd have expected to sound like their parents.

"Don't look at me like that, you know I love the dykey artsy types."

Mocha couldn't keep the heat from her face.

When Cora straightened and tossed her hair coyly like that, she looked exactly like Aunt Elsie did when she went on about her gay gardener.

Mocha wondered in no small horror if someday she'd be exactly like *her* mom. Begging to do her adult daughter's laundry just to feel useful. Scuffling sweetly around in some smothering husband's shadow.

"Ashley seems good at blending in," she stammered. "And I think she's photographed in a lot of churches. I'm sure she'll be fine."

"Well, and my mom *would* like pictures. All the great aunts and church ladies that'll die soon and all. Okay, go ahead and have her come!"

"Kay," Mocha said. Then she cleaned way faster

than she meant to and had an hour to kill before meeting Ashley.

She stopped at home.

Dad was working in the garden. Growing up, Mocha and Cora used to joke that he snuck out at night to measure the front lawn with a ruler and sleep beside his beds of flowers.

"Hey, Mochi. Just got off the phone with your aunt Cindy. She wanted to know how your party-planning gig is going?"

"Wedding planning, Dad." She sat on the wicker porch chair and kicked off her floral Converse.

"Maybe you could help her plan the family reunion this fall." He frowned slightly. "Cindy says your uncle is planning to bring his... hairy friend."

"You mean his partner?"

He shrugged. "I mean his mid-life crisis."

What the *fuck* was wrong with her family?

Her little college had been religious, but at least people there tip-toed around the existence of gay people, rather than outright disparaging them.

Since she'd been really young, the ignorant statements that flew around at home made her face hot. Especially because it wasn't the boys at school that made her face hot.

"Jesus, Daddy."

He gave her a little *watch the language* look. He could say that sort of thing all day, but *she* shouldn't. Then he changed his tune. "Well, good news. You might not need those wedding-planning gigs for much longer. Warren & Warren is looking for MBA interns."

"Interesting." She stood up and started inching for the door. Warren & Warren offered a ton of professional services in consulting, finance, and law, and poached a ton of interns. Not that they weren't prestigious. But they weren't the direction Mocha was heading.

Dad examined a slightly droopy cluster of geraniums.

"I'll bet I could get them to give you an interview."

"Huh. Maybe."

She flew through the front door—and bumped into Mom.

"Mochi! Don't run in the house. I pressed your green dress. I thought you might want to wear it to Cora's bridal shower."

Mom hadn't known about the shower that took place today. She was on the church invite list instead. Mocha had just generally said she was going to, "A bridal shower" to escape the house with minimal questioning.

"Thanks, Mom. You really don't have to do my clothes."

She waved away the protest and pushed an armful of pressed dresses into Mocha's grasp. Holy moly, school couldn't start soon enough.

CHAPTER 6

Mocha used to spend her summers working at the Flower Box. Half a florist, half a coffee shop, the scent of blooms and coffee mingled delightfully. She waved to her old coworkers and to the new girl at the flower counter, who snapped her gum and glared like she'd been affronted by the greeting.

"Hey Ross," she approached the front counter. "London Fog please?"

"Lavender syrup and honey?"

"It's like you know me!"

He winked, and she instantly regretted being so relaxed and playful. Ross had asked her out last summer, and she'd grabbed coffee with him and then politely said she wasn't looking for anything serious while in college. She'd hoped that was the end of any hopes.

Ashley appeared at her elbow, making her jump in surprise.

"One espresso, please."

While they waited for their drinks Mocha tried to strike up small talk. "How did you get into weddings?"

"I studied photography at MSU. I photographed the elopement of two friends and I was hooked. I like capturing details that might be overlooked. I like making brides feel comfortable and beautiful. I like being around love."

"Oh, me too!" Mocha flushed, surprised at such a sentimental answer from such a stoic person. "I love the details, but what I really love is love. Just hearing everyone's story and being around couples that really adore each other, that's my favorite. Do you only photograph weddings?"

Ashley's order came in the tiniest cup Mocha had ever seen. It looked like an American Girl doll mug.

"And engagements and elopements. I sometimes do product photos, brand shoots, and I've done a lot of maternity shoots lately. I don't offer them outright, but requests crop up, especially from former brides. The only thing I refuse to do is family shoots. I was not blessed with the patience to work with kids."

"I feel that," she laughed thoughtlessly. "I'm so not into kids."

"*You* aren't into kids?" it was Ashley's turn to look a little surprised.

And Mocha was instantly on the defensive. "I think it's because everyone expects me to be the mom type.

And I'm not. Don't repeat that."

"You don't have to apologize! You're allowed to not like kids. I love my friend's kids, but I've never needed any of my own to feel like my life was complete."

Mocha rarely felt seen in this area and she rarely discussed it. Cousin Cora used to say she felt the same, but that *"maybe I'll have just one, you know, just to check it off the life list."*

The vulnerability caused discomfort, so she made more small talk while she scurried to keep up with Ashley's long strides. "You said you were born in Wisconsin?"

"Born and raised. We fled here in the middle of the night when I was twelve to get away from my dad. We still spent summers there, at my grandmother's. That's where I met my girlfriend. My mom and little sister moved back once Dad died."

Ashley sure didn't pull punches or waste time with small talk.

"They live in my grandmother's old house and I stay with them whenever I'm working Wisconsin weddings. I love Michigan, but Wisconsin feels like home."

"I've never left Michigan," Mocha said, settling into her seat and taking a long, warming sip of her London Fog.

"You've... what?"

She suddenly realized what a bumpkin she'd just made herself sound like.

She lowered her cup. "Well that's not exactly true,

I've just never been to any other state. I've been to Canada, though."

Ashley was still staring at her, uncomprehending.

"There's so much to do right here. When we'd go on vacation we'd go to Mackinac, or Traverse City, or Toronto, or a lake house, and all the places my dad grew up visiting. He said the whole world was right here."

Ashley looked like she didn't buy it.

Mocha cleared her throat awkwardly, tugged her planner out of her bag, and launched into work.

"That Mackinac wedding isn't until spring. They've booked Hotel Iroquois."

"Oh, wow. Gorgeous."

"Two brides. They are so stinking cute. I'm so excited," and she genuinely was, instantly in her zone while in planning mode. "I haven't done any Mackinac weddings yet. Here's their photography budget." She passed over a page.

"Holy Jesus. Well. They can afford me. I hope they're paying you out the butt, then."

"Well, not exactly." Mocha neatened her stack of papers. "Still building my portfolio and everything. Not charging big girl prices yet."

"You should. I stalked your website. You aren't a hobbyist."

Mocha tried not to look as pleased as she felt. "Thanks. I stalked yours too. Your work is... *really* glamorous."

Ashley shrugged off the cardigan she was wearing, revealing her shoulder ink. Mocha tried not to examine it too closely, but she recognized each of the flowers and wondered what they meant to her.

The tingles she felt for Ashley were undeniable. She'd felt them before. Most recently, she'd been entranced by the girl she sat next to in her content marketing class. Before that, there was her lab partner in Biology. Sofía and Molly. She still talked to them both. These days they mostly talked about how great their boyfriends were.

Her parents and her small-town life were all obstacles to exploring feelings for other girls. All she knew was that both Sofía and Molly's small talk and casual glances affected her more than any of the boyfriends she'd ever had.

She'd had a few lackadaisical relationships in town. All good, clean-cut boys, the kind her Mother grinned at when she brought them home. All of them sensed her heart wasn't in it and found a reason to break it off.

And so Mocha focused on her vision for her future and only thought about love as it pertained to the couples she worked for.

She'd been in this coffee shop for several dates and even a breakup or two and had never felt jitters quite like this. She knew she'd feel it and then it would fade when reality sank firmly in, just like all the rest of her small, secret infatuations. But she missed this feeling and how it made every day a little brighter.

And she had to admit, this was a little different. She'd never had a crush on a girl who wasn't straight before. She wondered how many people around here knew Ashley's orientation, because she could never shake the gross feeling that most people in Harper Port wouldn't warm to an outright lesbian wedding vendor.

"I'll set up a meeting with the couple then," Mocha said, scribbling notes in her organizer.

Ashley pulled up a tablet to show off some of the engagement party photos. It was like she'd photographed a gala rather than a party at her aunt and uncle's house. The lighting, the color, and the misty night were all striking. Cora and Mason on the porch swing looked like a still from a romance film. And Mocha flushed a little at the picture of herself, snapped so abruptly on the lawn. She was framed in the light from the house and the faint mist falling on the landscape. She nearly didn't recognize herself.

"I still have a few final edits to make. But you could swing by in a few days and grab the USB for Cora."

CHAPTER 7

In Ashley's house for the second time that summer, Mocha stared up at the litany of photos on the wall. Past-Ashley had done a wild range of things with her hair. Her locks had been blonde, pink, black-and-purple, and turquoise. In one photo she wore no makeup and she had a light sprinkling of freckles that Mocha would never have guessed existed. She'd worn her dark flowing hair cropped short, and all the way down to her ass. But no matter the hair color, or length, or amount of makeup, she was always visibly Ashley. And in most of her photos, she had an arm tugged around the redheaded girl.

"I guess I didn't mention last time. Her name was Tessa." Ashley appeared and proffered another cup of chamomile to Mocha. "Tess."

"Tess," Mocha repeated, not quite meaning to.

Tessa was stunning. Big brown eyes and wild scarlet hair. She was a real redhead, not the weird in-between kinda-red-kinda-blonde that Mocha was. She looked more woodland nymph than human, and in each photo, Ashley was tangled around her like ivy.

Some of the photos were a little risqué. She lingered a little too long in looking at one. Tess was wearing only a blanket, cradled against the front of her nude body. She sipped coffee, staring out of a sunny window, red hair spiraling everywhere.

Ashley noticed her noticing. "I'm planning to start offering boudoir shoots."

It was the sort of thing most people around here would have said with a blush or a hint of scandal, but Ashley said it like she was going to start offering chili cheese dogs.

"Tess always told me I should, but for a while I was too overwhelmed with wedding work."

"Has work dwindled lately?"

"Oh no. I'm just not balancing work with a relationship anymore."

"Oh."

She wasn't really sure why Ashley had made her tea if she was only here to pick up a USB.

She sat tentatively on the couch and sipped from the mug. Ashley sat too, swigging only water.

She wore a black tank top and a window was open to let in the warming June air.

"I love your tattoos," Mocha ventured. "Favorite flowers?"

"Birth flowers. For all the powerful, impactful

women in my life. Chrysanthemum for my grandma, aster for my mom, a daisy for my sister, larkspur for Tess," she looked a little bashful, "Cosmos for me."

Mocha absently rattled them off from memory. "November. September. April. July. October?"

She saw genuine full-blown surprise in Ashley's hazel eyes for the very first time.

"Yes!"

"I used to work at the Flower Box. The old owner was big on birth flowers and the language of flowers. I was his prize student. And now I get my brides incredible floral discounts."

Ashley warmed a little, into a softened demeanor that was also new. "Your birth month?"

"September."

"You'd be a morning glory, absolutely."

Some months had two birth flowers, and September was one of them. She flushed slightly.

Ashley broke her gaze and looked at the floor, looking sheepish. "For my senior project in college I photographed women and incorporated their birth flowers or flowers that meant something to them. I dug into the language of flowers in my written project."

"That's really cool. I think flowers are part of why I got into weddings. They make me happy."

"Do you have any tattoos?"

"Oh God no, my parents would murder me."

Ashley laughed, her sarcastic self back, but the warmth still lingered. "Because it's not like you're an adult or anything. Really, I can't figure you out. Are you an independent entrepreneur or a sheltered church girl? Which is it?"

"I couldn't really tell you," Mocha assented, and sipped her tea.

This was the longest and most naturally they'd really talked. And this was normally when Mocha would have whipped out her organizer or made some excuse to get down to business.

But she was only here to pick up a USB, not talk business.

And right now, Ashley looked as unsure about what to do with the moment of vulnerability as she did.

Luckily, her white cat came scurrying out of somewhere and intervened, launching into Mocha's lap.

"This rude boy is Tofu."

"Tofu! Oh my gosh, that is the cutest." She snuggled him instantly into her arms, and he put on his unenthused face, even if he had initiated this contact.

"You've made a friend," Ashley said wryly. "I'm gonna run to the bathroom." And she disappeared like she couldn't leave the room fast enough.

Tofu reluctantly came around to purring. He wriggled out of her grasp but purred on and rubbed up against her arms.

That's when she noticed a coffee table book. *Love* was the simple monogram on the front. She picked it up, hoping it wasn't a trespass, and opened the front cover.

Her heart melted.

It was an engagement shoot.

"Oh, Tofu…"

Ashley and Tessa were the opening spread, hands entangled, Tess's hand twinkling with an engagement ring.

She turned the page, to find photos of the proposal itself. They were by the lighthouse from Ashley's family photos and Ashley held a little blue box—and Tess covered her flushed face with both hands, visibly crying.

"Oh. My gosh."

The only thing that made her a poor choice for her profession was a strong propensity to cry when faced with obvious, profound, simple love.

The photos were taken in early fall, so green mingled with all the speckles of yellow in the landscape. In one photo Ashley kissed Tessa's forehead, holding her close in a tartan blanket.

God, they looked so in love.

Mocha couldn't even begin to imagine doing life with your childhood sweetheart. And then losing her…

She jumped when she realized Ashley was standing in the doorway.

She was staring, blankly, unblinking.

"I…" Mocha wiped her eyes. "I hope it was okay to look."

Ashley didn't answer. "I proposed a few months before she passed. We'd have been married last year."

"You look so happy," Mocha sniffed. "I'm sure…"

She trailed off.

She didn't know what it was about Ashley that made her rattle off her innermost thoughts.

But Ashley's look was probing. "You're sure?"

She hesitated. "I'm sure she'd want you to be that happy again."

Ashley looked more than a little pained by the words, and she wished she could take them back. She did a lot of wishing she could take her words back around Ashley.

CHAPTER 8

Ashley watched Mocha walk back home. Tess's roses, in all shades of pink, were coming through now and lined her trek to the house next door. Mocha walked like she was trying hard not to look back.

Ashley had expected to feel something like rage, like trespass, to have Mocha rifling through their engagement photos.

She'd waited for *any* kind of ache to come.

But it just felt like a new acquaintance was looking at photos of an old lover.

The lack of grief was what brought the grief.

She went to her room and cried, choked with guilt. She knew in her deepest heart of hearts that she thought of Tess constantly these days *trying* to feel her former heartache. But all she could feel was memory, love, tenderness, and a distinct lack of her.

That was scarier than seeing her ghost everywhere.

She tried to text her mom, her sister. But she didn't know what to say to either.
She settled on a message to Mom.

When Grandma died, did you feel like it was wrong of you to get on with your life?

Grandma wouldn't have wanted me to stop living.

It was tragic, losing a grandmother or a mother, but it was just different to lose your almost-wife. You didn't go pick out a new mother. It didn't feel like sickening unfaithfulness to live a life after losing her.
A second text came through. *Do you need to talk?*
What was she so broken up about? Mocha was pretty much a coworker, a sheltered, sweet, pretty girl, who was straight as far as she knew. She hadn't flirted, she hadn't conveyed any interest.
All she was panicking over was the feeling that *maybe* she could be interested in somebody new.
At Christmastime when she'd slept with Dani, the girl from Lansing, she'd been messed up for days. She consoled herself that it was only a hookup. She'd been lonely and Dani had been lonely, and they'd comforted each other. They'd never spoken again after that. Or more accurately, Ashley had never answered her calls.
There had been no reason to come unglued then and there was no reason to come apart now.

A third text came in.

Tess would want you to live a beautiful life, Ashley. And she'd want you to share it with someone if you wanted to.

The strangest impulse hit Ashley when she walked by the Flower Box.

It was one of those golden mornings that feels suspended from the rest of time, and the scent of flowers and coffee tangled in the light.

In that strangest suspended moment, she didn't resist the impulse.

She stepped through the blue door and was hit with an even stronger wave of roses, lilacs, and coffee. She stopped by the front counter for a double espresso, before heading to the florist counter in the back.

The girl there looked at her like she was sizing her up. Luckily, the manager swept over before she had to deal with the teenager.

"Good morning! Anything I can get you?"

"You do deliveries, yes?"

"We do!"

"I'll look around for a minute. Thanks."

She smelled several bouquets and planter pots. They were all lovely, the bright and bouncy daisies, the sweet peonies, and the frilly carnations, but none were quite right.

She found what she was looking for in the back of a floral refrigerator.

Ranunculus. Bright. Bouncy. Spirited. Colorful. Lovely. And in the language of flowers: *I find you charming.*

She didn't know what in the world drove the impulse so fiercely, only that she was committed to it now.

She went back to the counter. "Could I get a bouquet of ranunculus in those colors delivered to this address?" She put her phone on the counter, with the address she had copied from one of the many documents Mocha had passed her way.

"Oh, I know the place! Would you like to leave a note?"

"Yes please," she said quickly. She was sure Mocha wouldn't like her old coworkers speculating she had a secret admirer.

So all she put was, *Thanks for thinking of me for the Mackinac job.*

Then she went on with her day, a few errands, and then the usual drove of endlessly editing photos.

As the day dissolved into twilight her phone buzzed.

It was an unknown number.

Hey, it's Mocha. Pulled this number from the vendor info you gave me.

The flowers made my whole day.

She nearly struck up a conversation, but at the last second, she settled for,

I'm so glad. See you at Bridal Shower Pt. II.

CHAPTER 9

Mocha fired off a text to Ashley. *Finished setting up the grandma shower early and am running to the Flower Box. Want a coffee?*

I'd kill for an espresso. Ran out of time this morning.

Milk or sugar?

Um no lmao.

Mocha drove the rainy roads to Flower Box and ordered a large Irish Fog for herself. She'd never ordered an espresso in her life and stared in awe at the itty bitty 4-ounce to-go cup it came in. She doubled back. "Could I maybe order a second one?" Something felt wrong about presenting Ashley with only a thimble of coffee.

She left cradling a drink tray with one giant tea and two minuscule coffees.

If she was honest, she was anxious about this day. She hoped to God the church ladies would behave.

Ashley had arrived and had been let into the church to take detail shots. The festivities for this party were a lot tamer. No lingerie cupcakes and no alcohol. Just diamond ring cookies, bottles of sparkling cider with decorative floral labels from Etsy, and pastel décor everywhere with innocent sayings.

One read: *First comes love, then comes marriage, then…????*

Ah, yes, good old-fashioned church peer pressure to reproduce.

"You're a saint," Ashley grinned, taking both bitty espressos.

Mocha wished her grin wasn't so enticing.

"I hope you enjoy both sips."

She laughed, and Mocha felt like she'd just accomplished a delicious feat. Then Ashley leaned in and whispered, "Some church ladies are here a whole ass hour early, and each of them has already asked me if I have a boyfriend. Do you think if I said, 'Yes, and his name is Stephanie,' they'd get the picture?"

"Noooooo," Mocha said. "They'd just go, 'aww, he sounds like a nice young man with a grotesquely modern name. The downfall of the American family you know, gender fluid names.'"

Ashley snorted a laugh again and went to photograph the cake.

Mocha stood still for a moment, reveling in the

feeling of authentic banter with someone who felt so wildly out of reach. Then she took a long sip of tea to clear her head and launched back into working mode.

Cora arrived, sporting a lovely lacy dress, looking like a maidenly saint herself. She looked less enthused than at her previous party. "I have a whole gaggle of aunts hot on my trail. Let's get this over with!"

And sure enough, the aunts, great aunts, and grandmas came, led by Cora's mom and Mocha's mom, cradling twice as many gift bags of cooking utensils as the younger crowd.

She knew no one was hornier or more interested in the sex lives of other people than old ladies and had a feeling that panties and sex manuals were crammed into those gift bags as well.

She noticed Mom noticing Ashley as she photographed the growing stack of pastel-packaged presents. She didn't know why she felt a small panicked flutter, like her two worlds were about to collide, or why it suddenly felt so important that her mother like Ashley.

"Mom! This is the wedding photographer. She's our next-door neighbor."

Mom's eyes doubled in size. "Lands' sakes, I thought you looked familiar!"

Ashley warmly shook her hand. "Ashley Montez. Good to meet you. Mocha says she gets her mad organizational skills from you."

Mom flushed. It had been the right thing to say. "Oh no. She gets all that from her father."

"That's not what Mocha says. She showed me the

pies you made for her friend's fall elopement reception and they were gorgeous."

Mom was thrilled. "You are too sweet. No wonder Mocha's talked so much about you!"

"Mom!" Mocha blurted. She hadn't. Had she? She'd mentioned a new photographer contact once or twice, each time guessing it fell upon uncaring ears. "Yes," she said quickly. "She's a great photographer, I'm happy I've found her. Now you should go get cake."

The cake design they'd picked was a towering pink floral concoction that looked more like a baby-girl cake than a bridal one, and already the church ladies were cutting and serving.

They sat around the ancient folding tables and had Mocha to thank for the dainty lace and gold tablecloths because the ones they'd supplied were triple-used pink plastic ones.

And apparently, this was the summer of backwards-topia, because the malicious holy gossip started immediately.

"Did you hear Sally's son Stephen is dating a *man?* Named *Steve?*"

"Stephen and Steve, good heavens."

"What a waste."

"I think it's just to get back at his father. Wouldn't let him throw his life away and study art."

Mocha felt instant nausea.

Ashley stopped photographing and stared blankly like she couldn't believe she was hearing this unfold in real-time. Mocha's heart went a mile a minute but before she could change the subject one woman tried to talk to Ashley. "What church do you go to, young lady?"

"My family's Roman Catholic," she said quietly. It was enough to shut her Protestant ass down, and she didn't try to talk to Ashley again.

Then the reproductive-planning prying started.

"So, how many kids are you thinking, Cora?"

"Oh," she looked a little uncomfortable, and Cora was the queen of playing things off. Mocha knew full well that Cora didn't want kids right away, if ever. She still held loosely onto *maybe one day, just one*. "I don't know. I never had a hard, fast number."

"Well, how many does Mason want?"

"He liked being an only child. So, one or less."

"Less?" The ladies roared with laughter like that was a totally comical thought.

One of the matriarchs of the group spoke up. "Did you hear about poor Sarah Manley?"

Several of the women nodded grimly, some looked on in open curiosity.

"Well, keep her in your thoughts and prayers," the woman explained, the pro way to say, *'I'm about to gossip, but it's so you can pray for them, so it's a-okay.'*

"She went to the lady doctor just to make sure everything was all right before she married Daniel, you know, Betty's son. And, well, you know how the Manley family is, they aren't big on modern medicine, and none of them realized that Sarah had never gotten her period. Turns out, she was born without a uterus."

She dabbed her eyes with a napkin.

Ashley looked on in open horror. Her eyes were alarmingly expressive, at least to Mocha, and she read whole sentences in them. *Are we really talking about a woman's medical condition in front of everyone? How is this any of our business? What the fuck kind of bridal shower topic? What the fuck is happening?*

The woman snuffled, coughed, and went on. "Daniel is an upstanding young man. He says he'll marry her anyway. No children and all. Can you imagine? Just... an absolutely incredible man. No one would blame him if he walked away. His own mother told him that, we've all told him, but he's determined. Just a truly incredible man."

Ashley blinked rapidly and looked like she was swallowing back bile.

Cora swigged her sparkling cider like she wished it had alcoholic content.

When Ashley briefly glanced at Mocha, as if to gauge how she felt about all this, her eyes again spoke volumes. *Imagine, a world where somebody could love someone for something more than their uterus. Some men are just heroes that way.*

Mocha wished she could do anything other than wilt.

What was most sinking of all was how Mocha knew full well she'd sat silently around this kind of talk all her life. Ashley's presence, as an openly gay woman, who no doubt believed in silly little modern ideas like bodily autonomy, only served to highlight how awful it all was.

Mocha had found more progressive faith

communities after high school and was relieved to know they existed. But what Mom and Dad both didn't know was that church wasn't a regular part of her college life, and this sort of garbage was the reason why.

Ashley cleared her throat and went to photograph... something. Anything. She snapped absent photos of some of the flower arrangements she'd already gotten multiple pictures of.

Mocha called the shop just before closing.

"Hey, Marge. It's Mocha."

"Mocha! Did you like that bouquet the photographer sent you? I assume it was for you!"

"Yes," she cleared her throat. "We've been working together a lot. I wanted to send her back some for helping me out with a project?"

"Lovely idea, we just got in some stunning pink roses and—"

"Um," she interjected quietly, nervously. "Last time I was there I saw a few planter pots of blue salvia. Do you still have any?"

Mysterious, hardy, and standing tall. And they said exactly what she was feeling at the moment, even if it was a secret she'd hardly admitted to herself.

"We have one left!"

"Oh, perfect. Could you send them to—"

"We already have the address on file. Do you want to send a note?"

"Yes, please. If you could just put," She faltered. "*Sorry you had to be there for all that today.*" She couldn't think what else to say. "And sign my name."

"I'll drop these by with my last deliveries of the night."

CHAPTER 10

Ashley had to look up what blue salvia meant.

I think of you.

It could be a complete coincidence that of all the flowers in all the shop, Mocha had chosen them. But it made Ashley's heart skip the tiniest beat.

She didn't have a type, but if she did, Mocha was so far from it.

She did tend to be drawn to ambitious girls, shy girls who were fun and playful when they warmed up to you, and maybe, girls who liked a slightly dominant partner in bed. She did like to take the lead in bed.

And yes, when Mocha wasn't in wedding planner mode she had that *take me and dominate me* vibe for days.

But even still. *Quiet-warrior-goddess* was how she'd

describe the few lovers she'd had, and *repressed-and-probably home-schooled* would have fit Mocha much better.

Today she was shooting the Claire Morris and Bradley Green wedding, and Mocha was their planner. She tried to stem her small flutters of anticipation.

Mocha was stunning that morning.

She was always stunning, but the spring green of her dress brought out the green in her eyes, and the red-golden hair she normally wore up in some form or another was straightened and falling in a sunrise-colored waterfall down her shoulders.

And then she gave that apprehensive but warm smile she saved for Ashley.

Fuck, she was gorgeous. But you'd have to be an idiot not to see that. Ashley was sure she wasn't unique in her attraction to Mocha.

And maybe plain old-fashioned attraction was all there was to it. Maybe it was just a wave of lonely horniness like her Christmas fling, and it would pass, and it was nothing of life-shattering implications to worry about.

Mocha was professional as hell. "The bride has a specific request for detail shots."

"Lay it on me."

"She wants," she could see Mocha slightly cringe. "Everything laid out on the barn floor."

"Kay. I can do that."

"Oh, you haven't seen the barn floor."

The barn floor was jagged and ancient, riddled with slats, holes, and cracks for things to fall into. It was also where the ceremony was taking place, so this was going to be one creaky wedding.

"Well. It'll be vintage all right. What's happening here?"

Two groomsmen were on their knees on the floor, looking closely at it.

"We dropped the rings!"

"You did *what?*" Mocha snapped.

"She told us to bring them out here and lay them out for the photographer and they fell through the fucking floor."

Mocha looked unamused, but not panicked.

She clomped away on her impressively high heels and yanked a small black case out of her tote bag.

"Step aside please." The groomsmen obediently skittered away.

She knelt on the craggy wooden floor, elegant dress and all, and produced a fishing line and a fish hook.

Ashley was sure the disbelief trickled onto her face. "Do you always carry those around?"

"You would not believe how many weddings could be saved with fishing line. Or a hook. Daddy's fishing lessons finally coming in handy."

She tugged her phone out of a surprise dress pocket and flicked on the flashlight. Then she slowly lowered the hook and line, tongue sticking out while she concentrated.

"Ring one!" she said, plucking up the engagement ring. "Wedding band and groom's ring to go."

She made short work of them both.

"Thank you, gentlemen. You should probably go start getting ready. Ashley will join you all in a minute."

They fled like obedient children.

"Wow. I don't think I've ever seen anything so attractive."

Mocha blushed and then she laughed. "I've done much crazier things. I didn't even have to tie my skirt up for this emergency." She carefully laid the rings out on a long piece of lace. "Let me know if they run away again." And she left Ashley to do what she did best.

Detail shots were among Ashley's favorites.

Arranging the invitations, stationery, jewelry, and flowers in the quiet morning air, well before the chaos was underway, was deliciously soothing. Sometimes brides had requests like this but she mostly had a lot of freedom, and she'd photographed details in every backdrop from uniquely tiled bathroom floors to up in trees.

She finished photographing against the barn floor, and then she took some artistic liberties with the pine trees just outside, laying the bride's necklace and earrings in the boughs and the morning light.

She was in her zone, very much Zen, and enjoying the warm June morning, when she heard it.

A bellow that sounded like a dying cow.

The bellow was followed by a grunt that sounded like a cow being hit by a train.

Across the barnyard, she saw Mocha freeze in her tracks and they silently exchanged *what the fuck* faces.

Mocha started crunching off in the direction of the sound and Ashley followed.

They found a cowshed with a whole bundle of cows in it, one of them in a stall. She had wide eyes and visible distress.

She was bellowing unpleasantly.

"Um, excuse me?" Mocha called to a farmhand. "Um, hi. I'm the wedding planner."

He tipped the brim of his trucker cap.

"Is this cow actively giving birth?"

"Probably about to start."

Mocha's eyes widened. "Like right now?"

"Sure looks like it."

The poor cow grunted.

"Jesus H Christ," Mocha gasped. "Can she do that literally anywhere else?"

Ashley had never seen quite this fierce side of Mocha, and she was battling back a wild laugh.

The farmhand looked insulted. "Now, how would you feel if someone burst into your delivery room, looked at you with disgust, and said JESUS H CHRIST can you just do that somewhere else?"

Ashley fought really hard not to laugh.

"Point taken. I think." Mocha tried a different tack. "Well, I don't know if anybody told you, but we're about to have a wedding here, and a birthing cow could severely dampen the romantic mood."

"I'll be sure to take it up with the cow."

"Okay," Mocha's voice said she'd had enough of this. "Is there anywhere else we can move her to before she starts popping a calf?"

"I guess you could try moving her to the old barn up by the original house. If she'll let you."

Mocha's face was sheer disbelief, but the extremely useful young man gestured in the direction of the halters and lead ropes and went back to mucking out straw.

"Once she's on her side she's not going anywhere," he warned.

"Oh. My. God." Mocha rubbed the bridge of her nose. "I knew I shouldn't have worn these heels." And she grabbed the halter and buckled it onto the cow.

"I forgot for a minute we weren't in Wisconsin because this is the most Wisconsin thing I have ever seen."

"Will you hand me the lead rope *please?*" Mocha stuck out her hand aggressively for it.

"We are really doing this right now."

Mocha talked to the cow instead of Ashley. "I'm sorry, Miss Cow, and I congratulate you on motherhood, but you were not in the bridal vision statement. Ash? Could you undo that latch please?"

Ashley took the tiniest split second to recover.

Only a few women called her *Ash,* and they were all very special to her. The name sounded natural on Mocha's tongue.

She tugged the pen door open and Mocha tugged the cow onward.

The cow, luckily, followed, although not without a grunt or groan or two.

Ashley snapped a photo of the pair. Mocha glared,

before turning her attention back to the mother cow. "I am so very sorry. But I am sure you would be much more comfortable birthing elsewhere. The company here is stifling," she threw a little look back at the aggressively unapologetic farmhand. "I bet you'd rather be up by the nice cozy old farmhouse."

Ashley wasn't about to stop photographing.

Heels-and-all, Mocha led the cow across the yard, through a field, up a lane, and to the old barn by the old house. Ashley rolled the door aside. The barn *was* quiet and cozy, and Mocha even took the time to pick what looked to be the coziest stall.

"There. I will send a more competent stable hand your way, and you will birth in much quieter bliss with no nosey wedding guests." Ashley didn't know, but the cow did look a little pleased with the quieter surroundings. "You. Are. A. Doll." And Mocha patted the cow's nose. She dusted off her hands. And then wheeled on Ashley, back to business.

"The bride didn't want any getting-ready photos until her hair and makeup appointments were done. But she'll be getting back any minute. You better run if you want pics of the room and mimosa table before the bridesmaids descend."

"You've got it, Captain."

"You are a queen. I am going to go wrangle the groomsmen and make sure they know they need to be dressed for getting-ready pictures in the loft. Be there in just a minute."

And her groomsmen-wrangling skills must have been excellent because not a second after Ashley finished photographing the giant *Bride* balloon hanging over the giant farmhouse bed, the mimosas, and the silk robes laid out for the bridesmaids, Mocha appeared.

"The girls are getting here. We can leave them to get into their robes and then pop back in for mimosa toasts."

And they stepped out into the yard to greet the girls and wave them in. The bride came last, stepping out of an ancient rusty blue chevy, and grinning like she might burst.

"Oh my gosh, everything's so pretty!"

"Sneak in here, girl," Mocha ordered, grinning. "The men aren't allowed to see you!"

She gathered up her *bride* tote bag and her cowgirl boots and scurried into the farmhouse.

Ashley dissolved into her work again, snapping photos of the girls in their silk getting-ready robes and pearls. She had them pile onto the bed for the iconic morning mimosa toast and snapped candids of them doing their makeup while the bride had the finishing pins and pearls put into her hair.

She did like it when brides looked really truly happy. Some felt obligated to stress out, some felt palpable uncertainty about their decision, and a rare terrible few were clearly more invested in the wedding than the marriage. Ashley always felt for each of those brides, even the bridezillas, but the brides that reminded her why she did this were the ones with that glowing certainty in their eyes.

She'd been so very ready to be married once. She

could imagine how magic it must feel to know you were choosing to be family.

In the mirror she was facing, she noticed Mocha. She was watching with rapt attention while Ashley worked. Her eyes glid once over Ashley's body and then fluttered downward, embarrassed without even knowing Ashley was watching her.

She had definitely been checking her out.

And finally, between the flowers and that steamy little look, Ashley knew this was not nothing. Even if it was only flaming lust or a first out-of-college summertime crush, it was not nothing.

The rest of the day hit every single one of the bride's checkpoints of vintage bliss and had a lovely lack of birthing cows. The pond-side reception was golden and the traditional rice sendoff concluded with the perfect kiss.

When Ashley climbed into the car, exhausted, the first thing she did was check her steps.

18,000. Holy cow.

Thoughts of cows made her snicker. And then she let her head sink against the wheel.

She'd stayed to help with cleanup. It wasn't at all a part of her role, but she'd wanted to linger. There was something delightful about working in companionable silence with somebody who had your same passion. She'd caught the faint strawberry scent of Mocha's hair and the scent had aroused her more than she'd ever have expected.

"You're lonely," she chanted to herself. "You're lonely, and you're horny, and that's natural, and that's all."

But she still felt the heady buzz inside from hearing Mocha's laugh, watching her march a cow across the barnyard, seeing her in that dress, and feeling her eyes on her body.

She tugged out her phone to text Riley, her sister. *So. There might be a girl.*

It went to *read* immediately and fired back immediately.

Might be?

I don't know. You know how I am.

Well, don't sabotage yourself, Ash. It's been two years and there's no reason why you shouldn't date somebody. See where it goes! Keep me posted.

Ashley rubbed her eyes. And another text came in, a long one.

Because I know you feel like you need it: This is your permission to enjoy the company of new women. You don't need it. Tess would want you to have it. If nothing else, just enjoy. Tess would tell you that's what life is for.

She flashed back to Tess's first tattoo. On her foot. *Savor.* Ashley teased her that it would draw foot fetishists and Tess couldn't stand that joke. "*Stopping to savor life is what keeps me grounded. And the idea came to me when my feet were in the grass. That's why it's on my foot.*" Ashley put on her famous okay-but-I-don't-buy-it face and Tess rolled her eyes.

She felt it again. The well of guilt.

Why was she the one who got to go on savoring life?

She tried to go home and feel appropriate pain.

But the pain was wearing thin. Like clothing that didn't fit anymore.

After crashing for a good 10 hours, she stretched in the morning sun, and the first thing she wondered was what Mocha was doing.

And maybe her mom and Riley were right. If nothing else, there would be nothing wrong with seeing what could happen, with enjoying Mocha's company. Their lives and worlds sometimes felt light-years apart, but she really did like her company.

She started her espresso machine, tugged on her computer glasses, and settled into editing.

Right after detail photos were the photos of Mocha dragging along a pregnant cow. She laughed involuntarily at the very first picture of Mocha's fierce face.

An hour later, she couldn't help it if she noticed Mocha outside, sitting on her family's wrap-around porch in the sunny light. She was scribbling in notebooks, tapping away at her tablet, framed in flower boxes and hanging flower baskets.

She sent off her customary conversation starter text.

What are you doing today?

She could see Mocha look at her phone… and pick it up quickly.

Getting organized for my next wedding lol! You?

I've been editing these for my new Dairymaid Model Shoot. For my portfolio.

She's already screen-grabbed a few of the cow photos and she fired them to Mocha. She could see her groan, laugh, hide her face.

Oh dear God.

This shit is big in Russia. Glam dress, hair, makeup, rando wild animals...

I don't think dairy cows count as wild animals.

I'm putting a unique Americana spin on the trend.

Make it stop.

You are quite the model. Loving how the wedding photos are coming out btw, sepia and all.

Oh good!

She sent a favorite photo of the bride's jewelry hanging from the sunlit pine tree.

I love this! And then, *You are very good at what you do.*

Ashley felt the same strange overwhelming feeling she'd felt about sending the flowers. A strong impulse she couldn't quite resist.

I do need a few models to build my boudoir portfolio. Would you be interested?

Undeniably, the thought of Mocha in lacy lingerie, behind her camera, was enough to send her pulse thrumming. She looked across the way to see how the proposition was received and could tell straight away it hadn't landed well. Even from here, she could see the shock in Mocha's big, innocent eyes. She faltered and didn't respond right away and Ashley almost regretted the thoughtless message. Mocha finally tapped something out.

I'd have to think about it.

Take your time deciding. No rush.

CHAPTER 11

The texts resumed throughout the week, and the next, even though only a bit of grass and a low picket fence separated them and they could have easily talked over the divide. Their talk was mostly about wedding things. Ashley had a weekend of shoots in Detroit followed by a weekend in Traverse City and Mocha had two weekends back to back in her college town. They compared pictures and tiny snippets from their weddings apart.

The ring bearer threw the ring pillow in a rage... This adorable couple wrote songs for vows... The mother of the groom wore a white dress and made a speech about how she loved him first... This couple had a Star Wars theme... No matter how crazy or mundane, the messages made Mocha grin.

And the flowers resumed too. Mocha rolled out of bed on a rare day with nothing to do but enjoy the crisp late-June air lifting through the window. She decided to drink tea on the porch and picked a rose tea from her stash. While the water boiled she glanced casually out at Ashley's house, knowing full well that at this point in the day she wouldn't be able to see anything through the windows.

The glass dollhouse had taken on a strange solidity. She'd been in its rooms and met the woman inside and it seemed less doll-like, less out-of-this-world. But it hadn't quite broken the enchantment. More than ever now she thought it was the prettiest house she'd ever seen.

She put her hair up in a messy golden-red bun and carried her tea to the porch—and there sat a vase of flowers. They must have been delivered the evening before.

Camellias.

White camellias.

White meant *you're adorable.* They symbolized care for someone and patience.

She hoped Ashley wasn't looking out her window right then and couldn't see how hard she smiled as she scooped them up.

The next day she stopped at Flower Box early before meeting with a couple. It was a weekday and it was quiet and only the gum-popping girl seemed to be working both counters.

Mocha's eyes immediately traveled to a wall of new floral arrivals and went straight to a row of potted morning glories. Ashley's words filled her head. *"You'd be a morning glory, absolutely."*

Morning glories meant purely and simply *affection* or innocent love. Blue specifically meant deep emotion, even if those emotions couldn't be named. Sometimes in Victorian times, they were used to represent *love in vain,* but she chose not to think about that.

She crept up to the coffee counter, where gum-popping girl was gum-popping.

At first, she was kind of relieved. She didn't want her old boss wondering why she kept sending flowers to another woman. She hadn't quite figured out why herself.

The girl looked like a teenaged Hayden Panettiere without any of the charm, blandly staring while Mocha approached.

"Just you today?" Mocha asked cheerfully.

"*Yuppp,*" she said dryly.

"Could I get the rooibos in a tea latte?"

The girl looked at her blankly.

"With steamed milk?"

"Huh. Next time you can just say 'rooibos with steamed milk.'"

Whoa, okay. Mocha nearly lost her nerve to order the flowers.

She handed over her payment in cash. Knockoff Hayden took it like it was dirty and inconvenient.

What was wrong with the kids in town?? Thinking that straightaway made her feel old. But then it hit her that most of her friends growing up had been just as pissy about being a teenager trapped in a little town like Harper Port.

She almost felt sorry for Dollar Store Brand Hayden. She also remembered that she didn't need to be scared off by a snot-nosed child and squared her shoulders.

"And when you've got a minute I'd like to get some flower sent."

The girl pretty much eye-rolled but she nodded, grabbing the rooibos from its shelf and starting on Mocha's tea.

That night when her phone lit up with a text her heart leaped to her throat. *Ashley Montez.* She opened the text but before she could read it Mom appeared. She was covered in flour.

"Hi, Mom." She kissed her on the cheek. Then she noticed Mom had her on-a-mission look on her face.

"Daddy was hoping you'd be home tomorrow night for dinner with his business buddy. You remember Mr. Kelvin?"

"Oh. Yeah, I do."

His son was Blake. Blake had been the biggest asshat in high school and still bragged about football plays from 8 years ago like they were the highlight of his life.

"And I hear he's bringing his handsome son."

Oh, nooooo.

She didn't want to talk about high school and pretend it was the best thing that ever happened to her.

"Dad is trying to marry me off harder than you are."

Mom snorted and tugged a leaf from Mocha's hair that she hadn't known was caught there. "Well, he takes care of us and he's paying for your school. We can oblige him sometimes. I ironed your floral blue dress and it's hanging up in your room. You should wear it tomorrow."

"Thanks, Mom," she said numbly.

"It's been a while since you've dated anybody," Mom acknowledged.

Oh gosh, she didn't have the energy for this today. "Just focusing on what I want to do with my life."

Mom always looked inexplicably bummed when she talked like that. But after a beat, she looked hopeful. "Well, you don't *have* to tell me about who you're texting so often these days."

Mocha opened her mouth to protest—and then surprised herself with swift aversion. "He's just a friend."

"Oh." Mom looked pleased. "Is that why you smile like that whenever he messages you? Well, at least pretend to be a little happy to see Blake tomorrow?"

And with a pleased little look, she finally left Mocha alone.

She crept out into the backyard and finally got to read Ashley's text.

I feel guilty, I keep sending bouquets and you keep sending me whole pots.

Well, all your flowers are thriving. I thought maybe you could use a few more.

Lol, because I have a gardener who comes super early in the morning twice a week, I suck at flowers.

Another message.

But I love being surrounded by them, so thank you.

That night she dreamed about Ashley. They were somewhere with a lot of grass, somewhere near the shore, just talking. And then the talking dissolved into kissing. And then kissing dissolved into Ashley's hands under her shirt, unhooking her bra, feeling her breasts. Ashley made no short work of stripping her and putting her hands and lips all over her body.

Her sleep was shattered by a phone buzz.

A summer storm had rolled in and she had left the window cracked so her lace curtains were flapping in the blue breeze.

She rolled over to see that it was 11:30 p.m. and the phone call was from Cora.

"Cora?" she answered sleepily.

"Look." Cora's voice was tight. "I know this is technically my sister's job, but like I said, maid of honor in name only. And quite frankly, her plans are shit. So, she told me to pick the location and that we'll make it happen wherever, which really means, she'll expect *you* to make it happen. And I'm so sorry Mocha, but, would it be crazy of me to change up my bachelorette weekend again?"

"Not at all." Mocha sat up and rubbed her eyes. "It's your wedding."

"Okay. I don't *want* to go to the city. I don't *want* my mom to come—who the fuck does that? I don't want all our freaking cousins—except you, of course."

"You know you don't have to invite me."

"No, I really want you there! Just not people like freaking cousin Janine." Janine's secret nickname among the cousins was Jealous Janine. Mocha was already privately dreading how she'd behave at Cora's wedding.

Mocha knew that her presence there would serve mostly just to preserve Cora's sanity, but no offense was taken. She let Cora go on. "I just want you and the photographer. But other than that, I just want my sisters and my close friends. Just my bridal party."

Mocha felt manically around on her night table for the notepad and gel pens she kept there. "Okay. Just bridal party. I love it. Small and cozy. No city?"

"No. Or, not exactly. I just want to get away to somewhere relaxing with good food and good drinks and fun things to do. Maybe a lake trip."

"Saugatuck?" Mocha suggested.

"Yes! Gosh, I'd love that! Do you think we could make it happen?"

"I'll call around in the morning and get in touch with your sister for maid of honor input."

"You're the best Mocha. And... I don't want you to feel like you're babysitting us. I want it to feel like a vacation too. So, don't feel like you have to hang around us the whole weekend, I know you like to be alone sometimes—"

"I'll be there to support you and make sure things run smoothly and I'll skip out on the drinking benders and anything that'll give me motion sickness," she promised.

"Gosh, you're so amazing. Thank you. I'm so sorry. I just... I would like to relax with my friends and have fun and just not be around all this fucking *crazy* for a while."

"I can make all that happen."

She went and stood by the window—and a light in Ashley's yard caught her eye.

Ashley was sitting under the protective awning of her back porch swing, rain and all, staring out at nothing in particular.

All thoughts of bachelorette planning were completely derailed by a strong desire to creep out into the wet night and join her.

"It will be so amazing, Cora," she said, a little distractedly. "I'll get everything sorted with your sister and we'll wrangle the bridesmaids."

"Thank you," Cora sounded nearly choked with tears. "Seriously Mocha, you're a goddess."

She hung up and decided it would be too stalker-ey to keep watching Ashley, who was obviously having a solitary moment.

She forced herself back to bed.

When she woke she wished didn't feel like a teenage girl in love.

After a morning of planning a dynamite bachelorette weekend and feeling so useful and in her element, dinner with Blake and his father went about as delightfully as she expected.

They ate on the porch. She and Mom laid out the garden-themed dish set, and she spent the whole time resisting the urge to peek over at Ashley's house.

Blake referred to football games and plays she couldn't remember, class trips she didn't want to remember, who used to date who, who was with who now, who had babies now, and all the while their dads looked on like they were witnessing the first frays of real and true love.

Mocha was relieved when she got away and her ears weren't bleeding.

And all through that day and the next, she texted Ashley.

She sent her tentative plans for Saugatuck, Pinterest pins, and venue questions.

And by Saturday night, it was admittedly starting to get a little ridiculous, texting so furiously when Ashley was right next door.

Ashley was the first to say so.

Why are we texting about this lol you could just come over.

At that exact second Mom pounded on Mocha's door. "Sweetie, could I grab your laundry?"

It was 10:30 at night on a Saturday. Why the hell was Mom looking for laundry to do?

"Already did it for the week, Mom!" She shouted back, attention trained on her phone.

Lol, my parents will ask me where the hell I'm going.

"Next door to talk to Ashley." Or, "None of your business I'm an actual grown-ass woman."

Mocha bit her lip. Ashley wasn't wrong. She should be able to waltz next door if she felt like it. And if Ashley had been just any other neighbor or friend, she wouldn't have felt so conflicted.

But something about the abrupt request to come over made Mocha want to change into cuter underwear and throw on mascara, and that scared her more than anything.

She internally panicked for a minute before she messaged, *Okay, let me throw real pants on.*

And Ashley responded, *Lol, no pants required. I'm only wearing a sweater.*

Oh, Christ.

Before she could stop herself she glanced over at Ashley's house.

She was sitting cross-legged on her couch, MacBook in her lap, phone by her knee. And it did indeed look like she was only wearing an oversized chunky-knit sweater over underwear.

Agh, oh gosh.

Okay.

Mocha fought to get her pulse under control. She'd been around plenty of her friends in casual undress before.

It didn't mean anything.

Nothing meant anything.

She pulled a light hoodie on over her t-shirt, grabbed her phone and keys, and mostly as a cover, her binder.

Mom, sure enough, was patrolling the front of the house, looking for things to do.

"Mochi! Where are you going so late?"

"One of my friends needs to chat. Be right back."

Mom raised an eyebrow and was undoubtedly going to ask which friend, whether it was an emergency, if she needed the truck, if she should call in the Navy, but Mocha blitzed out of the door and down the front steps.

She *knew* Mom was watching to see where she went and in a moment of panic she kept walking right past Ashley's house.

She texted while she walked.

I'm sorry, long story, can you let me in your back door?

Oh my God. Did you have to sneak out of your house? Are we fifteen?

Listen, I'm looping around the block and coming through the back gate. Could you let me in?

You are sneaking out to visit me by cover of nightfall. That is so fucking cute.

Mocha did a lot of blush-grinning these days. A lot of irritation mixed with helpless smiling.

She continued down her street, turned right, and looped down the path that ran behind both their houses.

When she got to the back gate Ashley was there.

Her sweater fell to her thighs and Mocha could hardly help but stare at her graceful tan legs and think how lovely they must feel under your hands, or wrapped around you…

"You didn't use either of those extremely helpful lines I sent you?"

"It's just easier not to explain."

"Why? Are we planning to do bad things?"

Mocha didn't know what expression to put on her face.

"Are you going to let me in, or should I go home?"

Ashley smirked and flicked the latch, pushing the gate open wide with a seductive little look.

Mocha shuffled past her, keeping her eyes trained to the ground, and could *feel* Ashley's pleasure in her distress.

When they got into the house she saw that Ashley had been editing in front of a documentary. Audrey Hepburn. A projector she hadn't known existed splayed light and color onto the wall.

"Gosh, she was such a darling," Mocha flopped down onto the couch, staring at the still of Audrey.

"She was such an artist." Ashley sat next to her, painfully close. "I love people who bring things to life. I love capturing what people create. And what people are."

Her gaze on Mocha was agonizingly intense.

So Mocha abruptly stood.

"Can I make some tea?"

"Of course you can."

Ashley always looked so cool. She wished she could look half so cool in only an oversized sweater. She knew she'd look like a 90's child playing dress-up in her mother's clothes. Tofu hopped onto Ashley and she stroked him casually. "There's walnut chocolate chip cookies in there too, compliments of a pair of grooms. Their pictures are coming out gorgeous if you want to see."

"I'd love to." She flung open the tea cabinet… and there were three new boxes. Green tea, earl grey, and a berry blend. She tried to keep her heart from melting. "Did you restock your tea?"

She didn't look up from her computer or casually stroking her cat. "I hoped you'd be back around."

Mocha bit her lip and fought a smile. She picked the berry blend and put the kettle on, unable to quite look back at Ashley.

When her cup was made and a teaspoon of sugar stirred in she rejoined her on the sofa. Ashley had hooked her laptop up to the projector and pulled up a slideshow of the photos she was working on.

"It was at the Fox Theatre in Detroit."

"This is *stunning.*"

The opening photo was of the grooms kissing in front of the Broadway-Roaring-20's-esque FOX sign, all lit up in the smoky night.

The next photo was of the couple on the dance floor, inside the Art Deco theater with all its glittering vintage color.

"I am going to cry, they look so happy. These are so pretty."

"I'm so glad you love all this as much as I do."

Mocha tried to ignore how strong Ashley's hazel

brown eyes were tonight.

"You know," Ashley said, as she slowly tapped through the pictures. "I never asked you how *you* got into weddings."

She sniffed. "Oh no, that's *really* gonna make me cry, though." She set aside her tea and stroked Tofu as he wriggled against her hoodie sleeve. "I was in college. I went to a little religious college not far from here."

Ashley nodded. "That seems to be on-trend for local kids."

"I was always helping plan some event, and always accidentally ending up in charge. I had a good friend Charlotte in all the same clubs and activities. She dropped out after my first semester, because she came out, and you can only imagine how hard it would be to be bisexual, black, and out at a religious school. We kept in touch. And eventually, she asked if I would help her plan her wedding."

She took a long sip of her tea. Char's wedding had filled her with the strangest bittersweet feeling. It opened up a world of possibility where love prevailed and then bitterly revealed that such a world wasn't Mocha's world. Seeing how Char's family accepted her gave her such hope while seeing how her fiancé's own family ostracized her— a family from right here in Harper Port— brought Mocha hurtling back to earth.

"Char's wife's family didn't even come to the wedding, but they were so in love, so devoted to each other with or without their family's approval, and I loved that I got to be a part of that fierce commitment to love." She swirled her spoon, a little intensely, in her cup. "From there I was hooked. I just thought that love was love, and theirs was one of the sweetest loves I'd ever seen. And to be a small part of their love story and bringing their vision to life—I was just so addicted. I loved everything about it."

At that moment it clicked for Mocha that she loved bringing to life for others what she didn't think existed for herself.

She couldn't face Ashley, even if Ashely was full-on facing her. "So that's part of why I am so fixated on a couple's vision. I want them to block out the world, and focus on everything *they* love, focus on their uniqueness, and focus on everything that brought them together in the first place."

She looked sheepishly at Ashley, whose eyes weren't letting up. She was listening with rapt attention. "After that, I started helping other girls at school plan their weddings. And that's how I got started. Sorry. People's eyes start to glaze over with how mushy it all is."

"I love your ambition. And your drive. And your devotion. I think it's so sweet… and terribly sexy."

Sexy. She didn't think she'd ever been described as sexy before. Wholesome. Wifey material. Innocent. Charming, maybe.

There was a long beat of silence and Mocha tried not to imagine tangling her fingers in Ashley's long dark hair.

Ashley finally cleared her throat. "Technically.

Theoretically. Would it be a conflict of interest for you to date a wedding vendor?"

"No," she said cautiously, her heartbeat spiking. "I don't think so. A vendor is employed by the couple, the coordinator just hooks them up. In a sense."

Ashley nodded. And then she gave her a mischievous little look and inched a little bit closer.

Instant panic flooded Mocha's senses.

This was happening. Ashley was coming onto her. It was happening.

She wanted Ashley to kiss her. To pull her closer and do things to her body. But she still felt so painfully inexperienced. She'd messed around with boys but none of that felt real, and at her core, she still felt totally naïve and really truly scared.

She stood. "I should get home. My parents will send out a search party."

Ashley looked like she'd just been doused with cold water.

"I... understand. Thanks for coming over. I'm sorry it wasn't for anything important."

"No. I enjoyed it." She awkwardly put her cup down on the counter, with a little too much of a clatter. "I should just really get back home."

Ashley nodded, standing stiffly. "Back door?"

"Hmm?"

"Will you be escaping through the back door?"

"Oh. Yes. I probably should. Go back the way I came."

God, how awkward.

Ashley walked her to the back gate and watched

through the window to be sure she made it back to her parent's front door. Mocha waved a shaky goodbye from the porch and was relieved there were no perceivable hard feelings when Ashley waved back.

Ashley stood in the middle of her living room floor, staring at Mocha's empty teacup on the counter.

She had literally been opening her mouth to say, *"Can I kiss you?"* when Mocha shot to her feet.

And she'd imagined tugging her close by her waist, and kissing and nuzzling her neck first, before finding her lips.

Now she felt like she'd just talked herself into getting back on a horse and been brutally bucked off. And she was unable to think of anything other than Mocha's green, eager, *I want to trust you* eyes.

Maybe she'd read everything wrong and Mocha really was straight, but she couldn't shake each glance and laugh and look and moment. God, she couldn't remember the last time she'd wanted someone this badly. There had been so few girls apart from Tessa.

She had been really ready to feel Mocha in her arms, she realized. She was trembling, and there was an embarrassing dampness in her panties.

She decided just to text her.

Did I scare you?

No, I scared myself. I'm sorry.

Am I reading this all wrong? Am I making you uncomfortable, flirting with you?

There was a long minute with no response. Ashley sank into her couch and rubbed her forehead. She'd made a mistake. Mocha wasn't into her. She was probably shocked at the admission of flirting. She probably…
Her phone buzzed.

I like you so much, Ashley I just don't know what to do with what I'm feeling. She stared at the message, unable to help a small swell of hope, and then received another. *It's complicated. I just might need some time. And to think.*

Anxiety swelled again at the word *complicated*. An ex-girlfriend? Closeted? She'd bank money on closeted. An ex-*boy*friend? She was getting too into her own head.

Take all the time. I'd love nothing more than to spend more time with you, but I can wait, and I can get over it if I need to.

We'll talk more. Someday. I wasn't running away because I didn't want anything to do with you. I was running away because I did.
If that makes any sense.

I'm so sorry.

No apologies. I'll see you at Cora's bachelorette.

CHAPTER 12

Cora didn't smile the whole way to Saugatuck, and her tense shoulders didn't relax until they were in view of the Michigan west coast town.

Mocha knew full well when something was off with a bride, but she also knew her cousin. Cora wouldn't blurt until she was good and ready, and then she'd explode. So she kept her questions to herself and blasted early 2000's nostalgia songs in Aunt Elsie's minivan, a gaggle of five bridesmaids chattering in the back.

She looked a little like a chaperone on a school field trip, driving while doling out sunscreen and snacks with one hand.

Ashley was meeting them at the house they'd rented to photograph their afternoon of antics. Mocha had already made the almost two-hour drive to Saugatuck and back yesterday to clear her head and decorate the cozy historic house they were staying in.

Long drives kept her sane and were always a welcome escape when she had things to think about and the house buzzed with Mom's nervous energy.

Cora finally smiled when they pulled up to the house and the girls squealed.

It was a big blue three-story with a wraparound porch facing a brimming pond, a rear upper deck, and a sunroom.

Cora reached across to squeeze Mocha's arm. "This is so cute. Exactly what I needed! Like, an old lady vacation."

"Well, that's exactly what I specialize in."

"Oh, you know what I mean."

"I figure the top rooms are for me and Ashley because they're the smallest and we don't want to hear you raving above our heads. The rest are free game!"

The girls scrambled out of the van in real school trip style, racing to gather bags and claim rooms. Mocha took a moment to enjoy standing before grabbing her bag. A motorcycle's whir echoed down the lane and she looked up a little quicker than she meant to see Ashley pulling into the yard.

Mocha didn't know anyone who actively rode motorcycles or even seriously considered them a viable mode of transportation. She knew a few men and one woman who'd bought them as midlife crisis vehicles and then kept them in their garages. She couldn't help if she stared like Ashley was riding a unicorn. Or if she enjoyed the look of her in leather.

Jesus, she was a horny little piece of shit.

Ashley removed her helmet and took in the house,

the pond, the lawn, the flowers, and the gazebo. "This is pretty cute."

She hadn't seen her since the night she'd bolted, but no discomfort hung in the air and Mocha was happy to see her.

"Cora asked for an old lady vacation. That's a thing I could deliver."

Ashley laughed. "I'd stay here willingly." She dismounted her bike and unlatched her bag from whatever you called the back of a bike. Mocha knew she was staring, but the mental cue to stop didn't register soon enough.

"This thing you're staring at is called a motorcycle," Ashley teased, extracting a motorcycle cover from one of her bags. "Sinful people ride them."

"It's pretty," she said lamely.

"The fiancé loved bikes. And Saugatuck." She looked around her with the look of one trying to put on a brave face. "I haven't been for a couple of years."

Since Tess was alive, it clicked.

Mocha felt a lump develop in her throat and was about to apologize like there was any way she could have possibly known Saugatuck was special, but luckily Ashley carried on.

"Where's the bride? I have a thing for her."

Mocha waved inside and wondered how Ashley could pack everything she needed for a weekend, camera and lenses included, into those itsy bitsy saddle bag things.

Inside, Ashley handed Cora a *Bride-to-Be* bag. "You are my new favorite person!" Cora squealed, extracting a handful of shooter bottles in various shades of pink. Her bridesmaids were equally excited.

"Wait, you have to dig deeper though," Ashley prompted.

Cora rifled past the bottles until she found a first aid kit that read *Bachelorette Survival Kit*. It was crammed full of everything from tampons to Tylenol and antacids, a mini truth or dare game, annnnnd colorful condoms.

"You are seriously my favorite person ever." Cora showed off the kit, and Mocha was extra glad her aunt wasn't here.

While the girls were dissecting the tote bag Ashley realized the living room was decorated.

"Did you get here early, Mocha?"

"Yesterday."

"You have a small Type A problem." But she pulled her camera from the bag and started photographing the rose gold balloons, signage, and cocktail glasses.

"Well. Funnily enough, I got little wine bottles, and everything to mix every cocktail ever, but not little pink shooters."

"I dated a white girl for half of my life. They like pink alcohol and haunted shit."

Tonight's very first excursion was a tour of a haunted mansion. They normally only gave haunted tours for Halloween, but Mocha had somehow sweet-talked them into pulling one together just for Cora.

Mocha crossed her arms. "I'll have you know that haunted houses are inclusive spaces for *all*."

Ashley looked pleasantly surprised at her pushback. "You're right. I'm sorry for indulging in harmful stereotypes."

Mocha grinned and Ashley grinned and that's when they realized Cora was watching them banter.

Ashley turned her smile to the bride, who already had a glass of wine. "I'll make a group chat and get you girls pictures as I edit them so you have all the Instagram-able things."

"Mochi, aren't you so glad I found Ashley? She's the best."

"She is," Mocha said a bit choppily.

"Mochi and Ashley. The dream team over here!"

Ashley defused the moment by snapping a photo of the favors Mocha had laid out. She propped the rose gold sunglasses and the palm-leaf beach towels against a backdrop of bottles of rosé. She had an eye for exactly the sort of content they were going to splay on social media later.

"Well, ladies," Mocha spoke up. "Don't get too toasted. We have our haunted house tour in half an hour, and then it's to the bars!"

Cheering ensued and Mocha wondered if this was what sorority houses felt like.

They piled into the van, Ashley up front with Mocha, girls wearing their matching sunglasses and bachelorette sashes, and started making their way to the highway.

"Do you feel like a soccer mom?" Ashley asked.

"Yes. And we are going to *win*," was Mocha's quick response.

"Our daughter carries this team, though."

"Our daughter's back hurts from carrying this team!"

Ashley looked pleased that Mocha was at ease enough to play with her and Mocha liked the feeling too.

The girls were back at chattering and giggling and paying them no mind, and Mocha enjoyed having Ashley's attention focused solely on her.

"You've been here before, right?" Ashley asked.

"Not much. Dad had some weird aversion to Saugatuck."

Ashley nodded like that didn't shock her.

As the highway wound on Ashley pointed out a sign that read *Dunes,* with a pride flag hanging from it.

"So, way back when in the 60's you couldn't serve alcohol to gay men because elaborate reasons. But there was a club called The Blue Tempo, right here in Saugatuck, that was like, 'fuck you all' and nicely ignored the law." She let her hair out of its ponytail and Mocha caught a waft of its tropical smell. "It burned down in '69. But in the '80s one of their bartenders opened that place back there, and it became one of America's biggest LGBTQ resorts and it still is."

"I would never have had any idea!"

"But *way* back when in the 1910s gay men and women would come from all over for the Ox-Bow, an artist's colony. It's still a thing today." She sat back in her seat. "So. Saugatuck has a bit of a reputation."

Oh Gosh. Hence her Dad's aversion. She tried not

to wilt with embarrassment.

"I've had a lot of weddings out here. I'm sure you will too when word gets out you're an LGBTQ vendor."

Mocha flinched, but none of the girls in the back seemed to hear the conversation. She felt lumped in with a community she didn't deserve to be included in. When it came to clear-cut-sounding things like identity she didn't know who or what she was, only that some women made her heart and soul stand at attention and that Ashley was very much so one such woman.

As if sensing some mistake, Ashley quickly said, "Or, LGBTQ-friendly vendor."

Soon the highway crossed over Kalamazoo River and both were silent to take in its blue beauty, lined with trees and pristine buildings and docked boats.

She made a concentrated effort to focus on the road rather than Ashley, who was playing with the ends of her hair and staring out onto the gorgeous late afternoon. Mocha wondered what it would be like to road trip everywhere with her. Preferably without six loud women in the back of the car.

A tree-lined road carried them to the front of the estate, and Mocha pulled into the gravel parking lot while the girls oohed and ahhed at the sight of the mansion tucked back in the trees.

Ashley got right to work documenting the adventure. The mansion was prime for photography, and the girl's terrified faces, even in broad daylight, were highly entertaining.

Their riverside patio dinner had twinkle lights, leafy lattices, quirky sculpture art, and a view of the river, and the girls took full advantage of the photo ops. Right after dinner they found a gazebo by the water and it was all an Instagram wet dream.

By the time it was dark it was on to the bars. At the second bar, Mocha cornered Ashley.

Mocha was a few potent cocktails in, but Ashley hadn't had anything to drink *or* to eat. "Have you eaten *anything?*"

"I'm in the zone," she said simply, snapping a photo of a bridesmaid cradling a colorful cocktail, then just the colorful cocktail, then the group against the backdrop of river and bar lights.

The music was loud and the bridesmaids were sloshy.

"Kay, but like, you should eat."

"Thanks, Mom."

Mocha felt a flash of indignation at the dismissal.

"If I *was* your mother—" Mocha suddenly realized what she was saying, and that she was a little bit buzzed, and that she didn't know where the sentence was going.

But *that* made Ashley lower her camera and raise an eyebrow.

"If you were my mother *what?*"

Mocha lowered her lecturing finger. "Nothing."

"No. Now I want to know what you were going to say."

Mocha pushed a loose strand of hair back behind

her ear. "I am going to go get some water."

"Good call, Mom."

When she got back to the table Cora, who was more than a few drinks in, grabbed her arm and pulled her close.

"Girl talk. You and me. Outside."

"Okayyyy," she said hesitantly, grabbing a glass of water a split second before her cousin grabbed her hand and tugged her into the dark.

She pulled her onto a bench with a view of the water.

"Mocha. You are my best cousin."

"Awww, Cora."

"No. Listen. You are my best cousin, you're like one of my sisters only *closer*. And you should know that I experimented in college."

Oh, dear God.

Cora sniffed, sipped her pink-and-yellow cocktail, and went on. "You know I went to a real college."

"Yesss Cora, I know your school was so much cooler than mine."

"That's not the point. Although yes, my school was much cooler. But that's not what I'm saying." She swirled her glass of fruity concoction. "What I'm saying is I got to experiment, but I don't think *you* ever did."

"We experimented in Biology."

Drunk Cora looked annoyed. "Don't beat around the literal and figurative bush."

"Whoa. Okay."

"Mocha. I'm asking you straight-up. Have you ever

slept with a woman?"

Mocha could no longer play off the drunken line of questioning. Her face heated. Her pulse quickened. She could only stare at her cousin feeling like she'd been caught red-handed for something she'd never actually even done.

Cora lowered her drink and took both of Mocha's hands in hers, making Mocha's water glass topple off the bench. "Mochi. I made out with girls in college. It helped me realize that I was straight and I really did love Mason, but it was *empowering* for me."

"That's... nice."

Cora's eye contact was aggressive.

"Mochi. Do you think you're going to experiment with Ashley?"

"Oh. My. God." Mocha tried to get up.

Cora gripped her hands tighter and fastened her to the bench. "Because I think that you should. Or at least you should make out."

Mocha tried to look away but Cora reached out to grab her chin and turn her face back. "Because you guys have this badass-bitch meets good-girl chemistry for days and it's *very* sexy and *very* obvious. And I would *love* a dykey cousin! And even if that's not what you are I will love you and I will accept you and I think that you should do you, boo, you know?"

"Okay. Thank you. Maybe stop using the word dyke. Otherwise, this has all been so helpful."

"Mmm-kay. Okay. Good. I haven't told anybody else that I think this. But I do. You're my favorite cousin and you should do what your heart wants."

"Thank you, Cora."

"Yes. You're welcome." She launched forward before Mocha could even begin to process what was happening and planted a kiss on her lips.

"Okay. Well, this was educational. I'm gonna go refill my water and check on the others."

"You go Mocha. I love you."

"Yesss and you're coming with me to get water."

By the third bar, the bridal party was truly sloshy, and Ashley looked like she was running out of steam.

"Somebody should have told me to eat something," she said, biting into a chip layered in artichoke dip.

Mocha glared, and Ashley grinned.

"You really are lucky I'm not your mother."

"I am keeping in so many kinky remarks."

Mocha opened her mouth to say something back—and then saw Cora smiling smugly and contentedly at her and decided to end the conversation there.

CHAPTER 13

Ashley tried to ease her door quietly closed so as not to wake Mocha. She crept down the stairs with as much stealth as possible, hoping to enjoy the crisp July morning before it became oppressively hot.

She tried to quietly creak the front door shut and jumped in surprise to find Mocha already on the porch, a book in her lap.

"'Morning," Mocha greeted, a little shyly.

That shy-but-excited-to-see-her look was coming to affect Ashley strongly.

"I thought you were still sleeping! I was trying hard not to wake you."

"Sorry. I thought I'd enjoy a few minutes of quiet before people started waking up."

There was a pause then, as Ashley thought what a

perfect photograph this moment would make, Mocha huddled up on a porch chair with a sprawling green world behind her, morning light sifting through the flowers and the gazebo lattice.

"I was just going to see if I could find a coffee shop with a view. And something to eat. Last night someone reminded me I should probably eat."

"You should listen to that person."

"Wanna come with me?"

She liked that Mocha looked pleased. "Let me get my wallet."

They took off down the grass-lined path and followed the street, eventually coming to a stretch of coffee shops, storefronts, and eating haunts.

They found a cozy cafe where they were seated in a remote corner of the patio. Mocha ordered a chai tea and since they didn't serve espresso, Ashley got a black coffee.

Then they pored over the menus and sipped silently from hot mugs.

"This really is a beautiful place," Mocha said.

"I'm so glad Cora had you to put together a relaxing weekend. She looked like she could use it."

Mocha nodded. "I think Aunt Elsie is stressing her out. And Cora's sister was willing to up any amount of money for this just as long as she didn't have to plan anything, so it all worked out."

They lapsed into silence. Mocha looked at the menu, but Ashley felt strongly that her mind was on anything but. She seemed to decide what she wanted and pushed the menu listlessly aside. Then she warmed her hands on her mug and looked a little anxiously out at the pretty greenery.

Finally, she blurted, "Cora cornered me last night. Drunk Cora. She asked about me and you."

"Oh did she?" Ashley could feel her eyebrow arching.

"Yeah. Apparently, we have 'chemistry for days.'"

"Well that not *not* true."

She'd hoped Mocha would laugh and dissolve the tension but she just closely examined her pink fingernails and bit her lip.

The waitress came by to take their orders and then silence prevailed for another moment.

"Ashley. I'm still sorry I bolted that night I came over. I want to talk about it."

Ashley nodded and didn't speak.

"I am," she winced. "Really. Really inexperienced."

The earnestness of the admission only made Ashley want to scoop her up and hold her even more.

"What have you done before?" she asked, and then realized how painfully direct that was, and added, "You don't have to tell me."

"You've seen the way I was raised," she looked distraught. "I've never been with a girl."

Oh.

"I've messed around with boys and hated every second of it," she dropped her voice, even though nobody was sitting anywhere near them on the patio. "I've made out topless and I've had a few hands down my panties. But they were so rough and I hated it. And that's all."

Was that the only problem? Inexperience? Poor sweetheart.

"How old are you?" she asked gently.

"Twenty-four. I took some time off between high school and college."

She knew it wasn't that unreal, especially in families with such helicopter parents, for twenty-somethings to be inexperienced. But she and Tess had started their first innocent tumbles at seventeen, and it was a little hard to digest.

Still, it was oddly endearing. She looked so painfully adorable, struggling to admit all this like she wanted so badly to entrust herself to Ashley.

"I'll be thirty in a couple of years," Ashley said. "And... I'm definitely not inexperienced. Does any of that bother you?"

She shook her head fervently.

The waitress came by with coffee creamer, sugar, toast, and jam.

When she left, Ashley reached across the table to put a hand on top of Mocha's, and Mocha looked intently up into her eyes.

"More than anything I don't want you to feel pressured. If anything happens, I want you to be sure you want it to."

Mocha looked tense, like she was torn between desire and reserve and anxiety and hope. But she nodded.

And then her phone lit up with a text that read *Cora*.

"I should check this."

"Absolutely."

She flicked on her phone.

"Cora wants to know if we can go for a walk before everyone wakes up. Could I tell her to just come here?"

"Of course."

Mocha looked regretful that their time together was cut short. Quickly, she said, "I really do like spending time with you, Ashley."

"I really do like you."

She would never get over that adorable blush.

Cora arrived towards the end of their meal, looking hungover and sad. Mocha waved her onto the patio and pushed away her plate of quiche crust.

"Do you want a coffee?" She asked.

"Sure. I'm sorry to steal her away Ashley, but do you think I could grab Mochi after this?"

"Of course." Ashley pushed away her own finished plate of chorizo hash and polished off her coffee.

Then she dropped enough cash on the table to cover breakfast with a small wink that Mocha hoped Cora didn't see and disappeared.

Cora ordered her coffee in a to-go cup and Mocha ordered a second tea in the same. Then they walked, taking in the cozy morning quiet of the neighborhood.

Cora finally spoke.

"Mocha I feel like I'm on a runaway train that I can't control. This doesn't feel like our wedding at all."

Mocha had heard this sentiment from infinitely many brides, but always the Momzilla was unrelated to her, the family wasn't hers, and the bride wasn't her cousin. Instantly, her whole family and their barrage of judging eyes filled her head.

"Mom and Mason's parents have taken everything over. The colors are ugly. I'm going to be so miserable all day in that hideous veil and those clumsy heels. And no one gives a damn what I think about my own wedding day! And they're so good at making us feel like we're selfish for, I don't know, wanting to actually enjoy the day? I just want to get it over and done with now and I hate that feeling!"

They made it back to the house and stopped at the flower-lined gazebo. Mocha rallied herself as they sat down, reminding herself that this was just like any other wedding she'd been asked to plan.

"Well then. It's time to take back your wedding."

And she whipped her tiny for-emergencies notepad and mini gel pen out of her back pocket.

"This isn't your mom's wedding. This isn't our family's wedding. And if they are paying for it, that's a gift, that doesn't mean they get to control you. That's not how you give gifts, and they're adults, so it's time that they learn that."

She'd made this speech many times before, but

somehow it held new power now that it was her own family she was talking about.

"So, I need you to tell me everything you hate about how this wedding is going."

And Cora wasted no time at all.

"I let my mom talk me into a veil. I *hate* veils. I don't want to be wrestling with that thing in all my pictures and all through the ceremony. Plus. I think they're stupid. Mason knows what I look like."

No Veil Mocha wrote.

"And the cake we picked out is so fucking ugly! It looks like a baby shower threw up all over it, Mocha. It's *pink* and *blue*. And that's another thing! I let everyone talk me into blush and blue because Mom and Dad's wedding was blush and white, and his parent's was silver and blue. And now my wedding looks like a gender reveal. I hate it!"

Change the cake, she wrote.

Tweak the colors.

"And I wanted nothing more than to dance all night, with lights and glow sticks and my glow-in-the-dark Vans. Mom said she'd murder me if I wore Vans under my wedding dress and that glow sticks are tacky."

Vans

Glow sticks

Dance all night

"And since I was a little girl I wanted a sparkler send-off but of course the venue everybody pressured us into won't allow it."

Sparkler-esque send-off.

"And 95% of the guys on our invite list are freaking related to me, so I think it would be so creepy to do a garter toss, but *everyone* says we have to because it's tradition!"

Nix garter toss.

"And I *hate* the bridesmaid's outfits. But they already bought the dresses and my sister already bought the hairpieces and bracelets and it's too late and they look like they're going to prom in the '80s!"

Tweak bridesmaid look. Nix hairpieces and bracelets. No big hair. No prom.

Cora's eyes brimmed big with tears. "And it just feels so not me, and so not Mason. And now it feels way too late to change anything!"

"Well, it's definitely not." Mocha turned and took both of Cora's hands in hers. "Last time I was holding your hands, you kissed me. Please don't do that again."

Cora looked momentarily confused, and then she snorted. "Oh my gosh. I'm so sorry."

"Okay. Look at me. Breathe. We are going to make your wedding yours."

"But it's so late to change—"

"It is *never* too late to decide that you want to do things differently. You could be walking down the aisle and decide to do things differently. Or to just quit and elope! No one gets to control you. Not while I'm your wedding planner."

She flipped back to the first page she wrote on.

"Okay. We're nixing the veil. It's unworn and you can return it. And if you can't, I'll pay your mom back for it myself. Today we're looking at cakes and deciding what you actually want. It's not too late until it's baked."

She flipped the page. "Do you prefer blush or blue?"

"Definitely blush."

"Then we're nixing all things blue. Anything you want to go with the blush?"

"Burgundy," she looked sheepish. Everyone was doing blush and burgundy these days. It was the hottest color pairing.

"If that's what you like then that's what you get." She scribbled *blush and burgundy. Alert florist.*

"And… maybe gold if we could add it. I like gold way more than silver."

"Absolutely! And you *are* wearing your Vans. And you're getting your glow sticks. And I am sorry that we can't do a sparkler send-off, but have you seen fiber wands? They're like a mix between a glow stick and twinkle lights, and you can get ones with this really warm yellow light, and they create the same twinkly sparkler effect. They're magical in photos."

Cora looked like she could barely believe all this was happening. "Could we get something like that?"

"I can or my name isn't Mocha May Johnson."

In increments, Cora was starting to smile.

"Now we are *not* doing a garter toss, because yes, it *is* weird when your eight-year-old cousin catches it and grins like a little creep. And I think we can change up the bridesmaid's look without having them run out and buy new dresses this late in the game. I can get your sister to return the clunky silver headpieces and the bracelets and we can get some gold belts and jewelry instead. What do you think? I feel like it would modernize the dresses and tie in your gold."

"Mocha. How are you this fucking amazing?"

"And if your mom needs to yell at anybody she can yell at me."

Tears welled in Cora's eyes again, but this time they were happy tears, and she burrowed into Mocha's arms. "I felt like I was just always going to regret what should have been such a happy day. How can I ever thank you, Mocha?"

"By not listening to anybody else and marrying the love of your life and being happy."

Cora laugh-sobbed and hugged her tighter but at least didn't kiss her this time.

CHAPTER 14

Relieved to have everything patched up for Cora, Mocha couldn't shake her disappointment that she hadn't been able to carry on more alone-time with Ashley. Everyone was finally up by noon and she drove the group out to their first activity of the day: dune buggy rides.

When they unloaded the van, she wished them a good time.

"You aren't coming?" Ashley turned to her.

"I'll get motion sickness and throw up everywhere. It won't be cute."

Did Ashley look disappointed?

Mocha waved the group off and then got back into the van, excited to have an hour to herself. She found a coffee shop with a long line to the window, but the line was moving quickly and the guests looked happy, so she queued up and used the time to hop on Pinterest. She took screenshots of Cora's fresh cake inspiration and forwarded the pins to the cake artist.

With an iced tea latte and macaroons, she took up a picnic bench and scribbled in her notebook, *I think I'm really into Ashley Montez*. And then she scribbled it out.

If she truly, deeply, physically, and romantically wanted another woman, what did that mean for her whole life? Would Ashley be willing to see her in secret? What kind of a life would that be? If they went public would her parents disown her? Ever speak to her again? Dad would undoubtedly stop paying for school…

Her stomach sank and churned a little. She hadn't really allowed herself to think about that.

She remembered coming home in college and her dad blabbing to her mom that, *"Sherman's daughter is shacking up with some hippie, so they took her off their insurance, stopped paying for her classes, and told her that's an adult decision, and adults can pay their own way."* He looked almost proud of his friend for cutting off his nineteen-year-old. Mocha hadn't known whether it was another girl Sherman's daughter was with, but the idea of cutting off support to control and shame your children stayed with her.

Another time, in high school, Mom told Dad in hushed tones that one of her friends was devastated because her teenage son had been caught messing around with another boy. *"They sent him to a camp that they hope will straighten him out."*

Mocha had quietly filed all of these instances away and resolved that her parents would never know about the girls who made her heart ache, or that her first real crush had been Daisy Hollander on the volleyball team.

All day long she took control for other people. She took control of weddings and vendors and squirrely bridesmaids and unruly mothers, aunts, and sisters. But she felt like she could no more take control of her own life than ride a dune buggy without projectile vomiting.

She tried to turn on the fierce self that rose up when she was working a wedding, the self she'd seen in those photos Ashley took of her storming down the lane with a whole cow in tow, the self she'd shown Cora this morning, but she couldn't find her anywhere inside her.

She headed back to the dune ride lot to pick up the girls.

They were high-energy as they tumbled back into the van. One of them had gotten a little queasy so Ashley let her sit up front and crammed herself into the back, and Mocha felt the loss of her presence.

They were headed to a cider tasting next.

Mocha tried to engage but she was the designated driver and the few ciders she sipped kind of tasted the same to her. The girls were at 100, and Ashley was in the zone again with such a lovely location, but Mocha found Ashley's intense interest in the surroundings more engaging than the surroundings themselves.

They climbed into the van again and headed back to the house to get ready for an evening out.

As the girls spilled out of the vehicle Cora cornered Mocha again, but this time she cornered Ashley too.

"You two should take the night off."

"Oh, no—" Mocha started to say.

"Oh, but—" Ashley began.

"No. Seriously! It will just be more of last night, only sloppier, so we don't need any more photos, and we can catch a Lyft back. You two should just make some drinks and relax and enjoy the quiet. It's supposed to be a vacation for *all* of us."

She gave Mocha a coy little look. "There's this place I think you'd both die for. It's called Crane's Pie Pantry, Restaurant, and Winery. They have orchards and a winery and they cater wedding pies and I think you'll love everything about them! They do takeout too if you wanted a cozy night in. You can just drop us off and then head on your way."

They exchanged looks. Ashley gave a slight shrug of agreement.

"Okayyy," Mocha said. "If you're sure."

"They have a pie flight where you can try four different pies! You'll love it so much."

They drove the girls to their first bar of the evening and waved goodbye.

"So does your cousin work for this pie place? Because I felt like I was being sold a timeshare."

"I don't know but I feel like we have to go or she'll hurt me. I did kind of like the takeout idea."

"Yeah? I could go for an evening in."

Mocha didn't know why the thought of an evening in with Ashley made her skin tingle.

They called ahead and found the countryside restaurant nestled between orchards and pick-yourself farms. She'd have thought it was just a barnyard if not for Cora.

"Okay, this is kind of cool," Ashley said, once in the quirky interior. "Maybe we could do a pie flight while they're finishing our order? I'm kind of curious to know what a pie flight even looks like."

"Let's do it," Mocha said, her heart lurching a little at Ashley's eagerness.

The pie flights came as four little jars of pie on a sampler paddle.

"I hate when Cora's right," Mocha groaned, as she savored the first bite of pie. "This place is amazing."

"Do you have any stories from when the two of you were kids?"

"Dozens. I'm not telling you any."

"Wow. Really? There's nothing I could do to get you to tell me?" She didn't know eating pie could look defiantly seductive, or that you could hold such intense eye contact while doing it, but Ashley pulled it off.

"Nope."

"I can come up with an impressive array of goods and services to trade for a story."

Jesus, why was that face making her squirm?

"All right. You get me a jar of those raspberry preserves and I'll tell you anything you want to know."

"Done. You and Cora. Embarrassing childhood stories."

"Well. There was the time we were having a slumber party and Cora said she hated her stuffed elephant toy because she thought he was 'for babies.' He was tiny, think beanie baby-sized. She'd tried to throw it away, but her mom got really mad at her because it was a gift from our aunt Cindy. So. Important backstory. The week before I had found a leaf in the living room. My mom also had a candle in the living room."

Ashley had stopped eating pie and was very invested.

"I put the leaf in the candle fire. It was the single most rewarding experience of my child life, watching that little leaf burn. So, I shit you not, *I*, the little girl who never got into trouble or ever did anything wrong, looked at my cousin, and said, 'we could always set him on fire.'"

Ashley made a snort-laugh sound that was probably the cutest thing Mocha had ever heard in her life and covered her mouth with both hands.

"Yes. So. We crept down to the living room where my aunt always had candles lit. And we stuck Mr. Elephant's nose into the flame."

"What the fuck!" Ashley gasped.

"Of course, Mr. Elephant was primarily polyester, so the fabric did catch a little, but mostly his face just started melting. We screamed."

Ashley was in shock and horror, face still half-buried behind her hands.

"We dropped him because he was terrifying and also on fire. I started stomping on him because that's what I'd seen in movies. The sound of our screams brought my aunt and uncle running." She swigged her water. "So they arrived to the sight of me stomping on a smoky elephant with a half-melted face."

"Oh my God." Ashley's voice was choked with laughter.

"The only other time I got into that much trouble was when I let Cora cut my hair with Barbie scissors."

"Oh no!"

"Yeah. I will be shocked if that story isn't in my aunt's wedding speech. And now you have to tell me embarrassing childhood stories."

"No, I'm paying you in preserves. That was the bargain." And then in all seriousness, she added, "And all I can think of is the time my sister and I snuck into the neighbor's yard and tried to ride sheep like horses, but it was a *very* short attempt. Sheep don't like being ridden."

They got their to-go order and Ashley bought the raspberry preserves for Mocha and a jar of apple butter for herself.

On the drive back Mocha cranked up the radio.

"Oh yay," she half-sighed half-laughed. "Chicken Fried."

"Never heard of it."

"You've *never* heard Chicken Fried by the Zac Brown Band? Are you an American?"

"Oh no, I'm sorry. Is this on the citizenship test?"

"Come on, you're lying."

"Why would I lie to you about knowing this hick song?"

"You take that back!"

"Sorry. Why would I lie to you about knowing this very cultured and sophisticated song?"

"This is my favorite part too." She cranked it up. Ashley listened with rapt attention. And then she scowled.

"Did I just hear what I think I just heard?"

Mocha giggled. "Yes."

"Did he just salute the American soldiers... who gave their lives... 'so that we don't have to sacrifice chicken fried?'"

Mocha nodded past giggles. "And *jeans that fit just right.*"

"Oh my gosh, I hate this. I hate everything about this."

"You're not allowed to hate this!"

"Is that what we think the bad guys are coming for? Our chicken? I hate it. Turn it off."

Luckily the song faded out, and *Take Me Home, Country Roads,* took its place.

"*This* is an American song," Ashley assented.

And Mocha wasted no time turning it up.

"Oh dear God," Ashley laughed.

"I'm a girl from the sticks, did nobody tell you that?"

"I'm starting to figure it out."

But when the chorus struck, Ashley sang with her.

By the time they got back, clouds had crept in and it was starting to rain.

They spread out their dinner in the sunroom to listen to the rainwater hitting the panes and Mocha left the screen door open so they could smell it all.

"I hope the girls aren't on a patio," Mocha laughed, as they laid out their dinner.

"If I light some candles will you start burning various objects, or will it be okay?"

"I've learned to reign in my pyromania."

Ashley had gotten the salad with a side of toast smothered in apple butter, gouda, and honey. Mocha's veggie burger brimmed with pesto. They ate in a happy silence much different from the tense silence of that morning. Rainy air and low, warm contentment filled the gaps.

When dinner was over they blew out the candles and lit more inside. Mocha flipped through the books in the living room while Ashley looked through her pictures of the day.

"I'm going to fire some of these off to the girls and then I'm yours," Ashley said, putting her glasses on and flipping open her MacBook.

Mocha felt a tingle at the phrasing and internally lectured herself for being such a child.

Ashley helpfully elaborated, "We could watch a movie. Or we could make love in the rain."

"What?" Mocha turned quickly around.

"Hmm? What?" Ashley didn't look up from her work.

Mocha's face was burning, and she wished Ashley would look up and see her glare. But Ashley was not giving her the satisfaction.

She finally settled into a corner, flicked on a table lamp, and tried to settle back into reading her book.

She read the same lines over and over again and kept absently flipping pages.

Make love in the rain, she was sure that was what Ashley said, and she didn't know if had been serious or sarcastic or both but now she couldn't get the image out of her mind.

There was a damp heat between her legs that she tried painfully to ignore.

Then she felt a presence beside her and looked up to see Ashley, computer glasses still on, looking at her with a look that could only be described as tender. It made every inch of Mocha's skin warm.

She tugged off her glasses and put them down on the desk. "Will you come upstairs with me?"

Mocha's heart was in her throat but she slammed her book shut and she nodded.

Ashley held out a hand to her and she took it, marveling for the second time that day at how soft her hands were and how delicate her touch was.

She let herself be led upstairs and didn't dare breathe for fear she'd wake up. She expected Ashley to lead her to a bedroom, but she opened the door to the upper deck instead.

The air was like magic, and the deck's railings tangled with ivy and morning glories.

Once out in the air, Ashley turned to face Mocha, all but pinning her against the side of the house.

"Can I kiss you?" she asked.

She breathlessly nodded.

Ashley's lips were soft and her tongue was probing.

Mocha melted into her straightaway. She had never melted so immediately or naturally into a kiss.

But she had never kissed a woman before, either.

The hibiscus scent of Ashley's hair and the sweetness of her lips was almost too much to take. Mocha very deliberately pressed her body against hers, wanting more of her warmth.

When Ashley broke away Mocha's heart unraveled, but only for a few seconds. Ashley took her hand and pulled her onto the deck chair, where the kissing continued, allowing Mocha to huddle more deeply into her arms, and practically onto her lap.

She hadn't known a kiss could be so sensual, heightened by the scent of the rain and the flowers and by Ashley's roving hands in her hair, then on her waist, and then on her neck and then cupping her bottom.

Something in her lurched each time Ashley copped a feel of her bottom or arched so that her breasts gently collided with Mocha's.

"You are so lovely," Ashley whispered, letting the tip of her tongue find Mocha's.

She instantly imagined that tongue's wet softness all over her body, and then felt dirty for thinking of it.

Ashley pulled back, but it took her a moment to open her eyes.

"Do you want to make love?"

Oh, God.

A fire burned in Mocha's lower belly and she nodded.

"I need you to please tell me if anything's too much or if you need me to stop."

Mocha tried to form words. "I'm just afraid I'll be so awkward and make you uncomfortable and—"

"I can take the lead." Ashley swallowed hard, and admitted, "I very much like taking the lead. But I want you to be sure."

Mocha realized she was nearly grinding against Ashley with want. "I'm sure," she whispered. She was throbbing between her legs.

Ashley nodded. Then she took both of Mocha's hands and lifted her to her feet.

Out in the elemental air everything felt so primal and natural, but the minute they were in the bedroom Mocha felt a small sense of terror welling up in her. Ashley, who had probably done this a thousand times, turned on a low lamp and pushed the excessive throw pillows off the bed.

Mocha stood paralyzed in the doorway.

Ashley realized she wasn't beside her and turned to face her. "It's up to you, baby girl. We can just snuggle. Or I can give you time and space."

Baby girl. She could get used to Ashley calling her that.

"Maybe we could just snuggle at first? Just for a

little while."

"Of course we can." Ashley came forward and took Mocha's face in her hands. She kissed her cheek delicately and then led the way to the bed, for which Mocha felt profound relief. She'd forgotten for a long second how to make her feet move.

They nestled into the bed and listened wordlessly to the rain hitting the window, the trees, the grass. Ashley started to kiss the back of her neck, played with her hair, and let her hand feel out her waist, hip, and legs.

Mocha began to relax again, yielding to the gentle touches.

"You are so sweet," Ashley hummed quietly. Sensing remaining tendrils of apprehension she stroked Mocha's hair again. "I want you to feel safe."

"I do. I'm just… nervous."

"It's okay to feel nervous." Ashley gently turned Mocha onto her back and gently sidled on top of her. The heat between her legs spread to have Ashley straddling her, and once again kissing her.

"I thought you were adorable the moment I saw you. And then I got to know you and I wanted to constantly be by you."

She didn't know how Ashley had guessed that she needed words, but they were working, her body becoming more pliable under the kisses and caresses.

Ashley's hands roved up her tummy and forayed over each of her breasts and Mocha gasped a little, but not in protest.

The reaction seemed to hit Ashley strongly.

"Sit up, sweetheart."

She lifted enough for Mocha to do so, propped back against the pillows, and then straddled her lap again.

Ashley took off her own tank top first, revealing her black bra. Then she lifted Mocha's t-shirt, and though she shivered a little, she let her remove the top and take in the sight of her lacy blue bra.

"You're okay," Ashley whispered, in response to how she tried to hide her face in her hair.

Mocha mustered the bravery to respond. "You are..." she looked at her and then looked away. "So. Overwhelmingly. Beautiful."

Ashley kissed her again, only this time she reached behind her and unhooked her bra so quickly she'd hardly realized it happened.

Mocha hadn't been ready to be half-naked so soon and kept her chest firmly planted against Ashley's to avoid being seen, kissing her with a new urgency that had everything to do with her terror. Ashley sensed it and pulled back but didn't remove the unhooked bra, still very barely clinging to Mocha's breasts.

She reached behind herself and removed her own bra instead.

The sight of Ashley half-naked was enough to heat her all the way through. She almost reached forward to enclose her hands over Ashley's breasts, almost asked to put her mouth on them, but froze again.

She hoped to God Ashley wouldn't become frustrated with her anxiety, but it didn't seem to rattle her.

She inched forward to press her bare skin against Mocha's still-covered skin and kissed her neck. She had a way of kissing and nuzzling your neck that made you feel worshiped and adored.

Mocha was afraid she was being too passive and acted on her desire to reach forward and tentatively glide one thumb over Ashley's nipple.

Ashley shivered.

For a split second Mocha couldn't believe she had elicited that reaction.

"Very sensitive there," Ashley explained quietly, and then went back to kissing her.

But Mocha had been enthralled by the split second of power. She let her hand slide between their bodies again, and let her thumb again stroke Ashley's nipple, this time drawing a tiny circle.

Ashley shivered again, hard. And she grabbed both of Mocha's hands.

"You take care of everything. Please let somebody else take care of you for a little while."

"Okay. But. Then you have to let me."

"I will." The smile she gave made Mocha wetter with anticipation. "Can I take this off?" She ran a thumb over Mocha's loosely-clinging bra.

CHAPTER 15

Mocha took a moment to adjust to being bare. She'd been topless with a handful of boys before but nothing had felt as intimate as this, having Ashley's bare breasts press against hers while their kisses deepened.

She was throbbing now, her panties soaking now, ready in every way she'd never been before.

Then Ashley inched back down her body, kissing her tummy down to her shorts, then kissing her upper legs where her shorts didn't cover.

Then she grabbed her ankles and tugged her further down the bed.

"Oh my gosh!" Mocha half-gasped, half-giggled.

When Ashley looked up at her there was a playfulness in her eyes that quelled the panic that might otherwise rise up.

Ashley hopped off the edge of the bed and unbuttoned her own shorts and wriggled them down to her ankles, revealing simple black panties.

Then she clambered back onto the bed and began unfastening Mocha's yellow belt, making her breath catch. The belt had a stupidly elaborate clasp that took a second, and the button of her shorts was a little large for the slot it fit in, and her zipper pull was kind of crammed into the top of her shorts.

"Is this a chastity obstacle course?"

"Yes," Mocha giggled, forcing herself to relax against the pillows. "They teach you that in youth group."

"Knowing you has been so educational."

Ashley finally got the shorts unlatched and tugged them expertly down Mocha's legs and let them slide to the floor.

"Awwww!" Ashley laughed suddenly, at the sight of Mocha's panties.

They were smiley-face panties.

"That is," Ashley snickered. "So cute."

"I wasn't planning on losing my innocence today."

"Well, now I feel like a sicko. I've been thinking about you naked all day."

"Agh," Mocha buried her face in her hands.

Ashley kissed up her legs again, this time pausing for longer, steamier kisses that made Mocha's skin prickle. When her kisses climbed up to her inner thighs she began to tremble.

Ashley stroked the crotch of Mocha's damp panties and Mocha softly panted.

"Too much?"

"No," Mocha said, more assertively than she

meant.

So Ashley stroked her again, gliding all the way up the damp outline of her slit and stopping at her clit. She rubbed there, applying a little pressure. The feeling of Ashley's finger on her clit, even through hot fabric, was sexier than anything Mocha had ever dreamed.

Then Ashley leaned down and kissed her through her panties.

"Oh my gosh."

In response, Ashley hooked one finger under the waistband of her panties, still gently nuzzling Mocha's crotch through the fabric.

"Is being completely naked new territory?"

"Yes," her voice sounded hoarse and dry.

"Do you need more time?"

"No."

And Ashley reached her other hand up to seize the other hip of Mocha's panties, and slid them down her legs, to her ankles, and off.

She hovered at the foot of the bed a moment, taking in the sight of her.

"Fuck." Her voice was tight.

Mocha was really trembling now.

"I... really wasn't planning for this. I didn't shave or..."

"No, you're perfect," Ashley was already sliding a hand between both her legs so that she could part them. She couldn't see her expression, hidden as it was in her long dark hair, but her mouth was hovering precariously over her pussy.

"God, you smell amazing."

Mocha buried her face again with both hands and Ashley made a small noise that wasn't quite laughter. "I love," she whispered, "that you are so shy. But so excited." And she slid her finger over Mocha's wet, most intimate folds, making her arch and gasp. "You are *so* hot and wet for me, baby girl."

She'd struggled to get wet before for past boyfriends, feeling dry and tense and miserable but she was pulsing with want for Ashley.

Ashley drew her thumb in circles over her clit, making her more audibly gasp. Then she felt out her entry, and how wet it was.

"You're ready for me. I'm going to push into you, okay?"

Mocha didn't know how exactly she meant until she felt one finger nestle at her soaking entrance. She nodded eagerly, and then realized Ashley couldn't see her, her eyes focused intently on the apex of her thighs. "Yes. Yes please."

And Ashley let her finger slide into Mocha. She stiffened momentarily and took a minute to adjust to the feeling of Ashley inside her. Ashley kissed the insides of her thighs again, and she relaxed a little, drawing the finger in deeper. Ashley released a soft moan and began to build up slight friction with her finger, still giving time to adjust.

And then she extracted and inserted two fingers.

Mocha made soft panting sounds she'd never heard herself make and gathered the blanket into her fists. "Oh. Ashley."

Ashley seemed very fixated on how Mocha pulsed around her and smiled when Mocha began to tentatively give little thrusts against her hand. She fingered her for a long, breathless, suspended, rainy while.

And then, as if bursting with something she couldn't resist any longer, Ashley extracted both fingers.

Mocha released a soft moan at the loss of her.

"I… really, really enjoy pleasuring with my tongue and can do it for hours. Please tell me if it starts to be too much."

Mocha took a minute to process what she was hearing.

"I've never done that before," she admitted. "Or. I guess. I've given it before. To dudes."

"Well the nice thing is you don't have to *do* anything," Ashley's eyes were trained on Mocha's quivering womanhood. "Except maybe, clench your legs around me. If you want to."

She grabbed a pillow and lifted Mocha's bottom, expertly propping the pillow under it. Having her pussy so brazenly exposed to Ashley, like she was on an altar, was more than a little sexy.

Ashley flashed a devilish smirk. "And that means your first time won't be with some dumbass boy in the back of a Jetta. So it'll actually feel good."

She spread Mocha's legs a little and sank her tongue hungrily.

Mocha had never felt anything like Ashley's tongue in her life and released a small and completely involuntarily cry, which only urged Ashley along with more intensity.

She razed her with her tongue, swirling at her wet entry, arching up through her every dip and fold, and then glazing over her clit, and lingering there, swirling and licking and stroking and savoring.

She pulled away only long enough to whisper, "You taste so stunning," before gripping both of Mocha's legs and tonguing her deeper. Her mouth was warm and soft one moment, and hard and probing the next. She favored Mocha's clit and Mocha had to grip the covers again, to keep from climaxing in minutes.

"You… are… so… amazing…"

"I adore you," Ashley said simply, briefly, her mouth not long from Mocha's vulva. She let it glide in long strokes, and then quick, heat-inducing strokes, gliding low, and then gliding high to her most sensitive nub. She licked and sucked and stroked in intensifying waves, and built up the most excruciating friction Mocha had ever felt.

She wanted to cry.

In her most secret fantasies, in her stupidly girlish bedroom, she'd dreamed of another woman making love to her with her mouth like this. When she'd met Ashley, her most secret dreams had taken Ashley's shape.

But that's all they'd been. Secrets and dreams. Not a real part of herself that could ever be embodied.

And Ashley was right. This wasn't like the carnal car fumbles she'd experienced before. In every hot wet stroke, Mocha felt Ashley's adoration and earnest want.

She felt in her core that Ashley would snuggle her all night, would be there when she woke up, would bring her tea, and would want to spend more time with her, and she knew she'd want all of those things back.

And that realization filled her with happiness and filled her with the sickening thud of reality.

Did she think she could magically wake up and be Ashley's girlfriend tomorrow?

The thought made her tense up a little and Ashley, busy in her most intimate parts, felt it.

"You're okay baby," she whispered. "You can come."

The permission brought Mocha back to the present. The heat in her core *was* building, and Ashley's attention to the hard bud of her clitoris was starting to pulse in every inch of her body.

She'd never climaxed in another person's presence before, and definitely never *because* of another person. This moment felt like the culmination of giving herself to Ashley, of her first real and true time wholeheartedly engaged in sex.

Fear of reality was clouded out by the desire to be here, with the rain lashing the windows and Ashley's tongue so sweetly lashing her.

She yielded to the building wave of wet heat and tongue-caressing.

Ashley gave a long lick that trailed all the way up to her clitoris and it nearly pushed her over the edge.

"It's okay," Ashley said, sensing that Mocha needed to know that it was.

And she thrust her tongue repeatedly and incessantly against Mocha's most sensitive part.

She gasped and bucked against her tongue, and then she cried out.

The sizzle in her clit became fireworks, razing her whole body. She gave herself over to Ashley's tongue and accepted the climax and accepted that in this moment, this was what and who she wanted.

She'd thought it was silly to think your first time was what made you a woman, but she did feel like she was stepping onto a new plane of existence, in which she was finally a glimmer of who she actually was.

When the fireworks cleared tranquility flooded her senses, and then the sweetness of Ashley's face.

She looked a little sheepish at her own aggressiveness. "I'm going to take a minute."

"Of course," Mocha laughed, delighted at her own lightness, reaching up to brush Ashley's cheek with the back of her hand.

Ashley visibly melted at the touch before disappearing into the bathroom.

Mocha laid back and listened to distant thunder and the quiet hum of the bathroom faucet. She knew full well she'd have been too embarrassed to kiss Ashley with her own wetness all over her mouth and on her tongue and was glad that Ashley seemed to guess that. She seemed to think of everything. If her experience disarmed her, it wasn't off-putting. She blushed wildly, imagining what else Ashley could do to her, and show her, and found it the most charming thing in the world that she wanted to take care of her.

When she returned she wasn't wearing panties and Mocha sat up, feeling a rush of delight at the sight of her. All but a strip of her was shaved and she looked… surprisingly delicate and vulnerable, and even a little bit bashful.

"I didn't think it was fair for you to be the only one naked?"

"Well, that's sweet of you. And you should come over here and let me touch you now."

This exchange of boldness was exciting to both.

Ashley crept forward and sat on the edge of the bed, once more taking in the sight of Mocha in her relaxed, happy glory, before lying alongside her.

"Don't feel like you have to try anything you aren't ready for."

"Stop worrying about me. Can I touch your boobs now?"

Ashley grinned. "Yes."

Mocha wanted to surprise her. So rather than ease her way into things with her hands she lowered her face to Ashley's breast and sucked her nipple into her mouth.

Ashley lurched. "Holy fuck, Mocha," she gently grabbed a fistful of her hair and tugged her away.

"You okay?" Mocha laughed.

Ashley looked like she was about to admit something that made her shy. "So, fun fact, some women are *really* sensitive there."

"Mm-hmm?"

"And I am one of those women."

Oh, gosh. "Okay."

"So. You could probably make me come just by tonguing me there."

That thought gave Mocha chills. "Really? I mean, I read about boob orgasms once but I thought maybe that was something Cosmo just made up."

Ashley snorted a laugh. "Nope. Cosmo didn't make that one up. But a lot of people don't believe it's a thing. I definitely had a girl accuse me of faking it once."

Mocha smiled. "Well. This works out because I really want you to stop explaining and let me play with them."

Now Ashley was the one who hid her face in her hair. "You are my dream."

Mocha squeezed both breasts and Ashley softly moaned. Then she rubbed her thumbs over each nipple and very much enjoyed the aching pleasure-face Ashley made.

"I am enjoying this power," Mocha said, emboldened.

"You have a lot of power over me."

That knowledge was intoxicating. She wondered if Ashley had ever had hot and heavy dreams of *her*.

Mocha again lowered her mouth and gently closed it over a nipple and this time, although Ashley shuddered, she didn't protest. She savored feeling Ashley's delicateness in her mouth, and then she swirled her tongue.

Ashley moaned. "Oh. Please..."

Her plea was wildly empowering and urged Mocha on, swirling and suckling and tongue-flicking. Ashley vulnerably leaned in and whimpered, and Mocha could hardly believe this was powerful stoic Ashley, coming apart just from having her tit in Mocha's mouth.

Mocha gently pinched down her teeth and Ashley jumped. "God."

She returned to just tongue, resolving to save that for later.

She sucked and tugged with her lips in tiny little tugs that seemed to drive Ashley wild. While she sucked she let her hand rove to Ashley's thighs and then dipped one finger between her legs.

Ashley was soaking wet.

"Oh," Mocha moaned softly against her skin, stroking with both her tongue and her finger now.

Ashley's trembling was multiplied by the petting between her legs and the whimpering and moaning increased.

And then Mocha tongue-flicked the tip of her nipple.

She gasped and sank her fist again into Mocha's hair.

"I'm going to come."

Mocha only smiled in response and let her tongue work her taut nipple again, while her finger worked her taut clitoris. Ashley was squirming on the precipice and tightened her grip in Mocha's hair. Mocha responded by fastening her mouth more tightly to her tit.

She groaned and shuddered deeply.

And then Mocha pinched her teeth down, ever-so-gently and she released a yelp.

"Oh my gosh, I'm coming, I'm coming."

And Mocha swirled her finger on her vulva again and felt the joy of Ashley dissolving into climax against her hand.

She cried out again and pushed her nipple deeper into Mocha's mouth and came hard.

Mocha enjoyed every second of her coming undone against her, her grip in her hair, and how it loosened when the climax cleared and Ashley collapsed against her.

"Oh my God," Ashley said, her voice weak.

And in the quiet aftermath, Mocha didn't withdraw her hand from between Ashley's legs, just softly swirling in the wetness there, savoring Ashley resting vulnerably against her. "Wow."

They stayed that way for a while, Ashley breathing deeply, Mocha caressing her pussy softly. When Mocha withdrew her hand Ashley snuggled into her arms and kissed her long and deep.

They fell asleep in the rainy haze.

CHAPTER 16

Mocha's hair smelled like heaven in the sunny after-rain air from the window. Ashley burrowed her face in it and smiled.

Already her mind was swirling with the sort of thoughts she knew were dangerous. *I'm never letting you go* and other way-too-soon things like that. When she'd known with Tess, even as young as they were, she'd known, and she knew it now.

Thoughts of Tess didn't make her feel the expected betrayal.

Because of Tess, she knew when something was special.

And everything about this was special.

Mocha stirred with a soft hum and Ashley kissed her head.

"I'll drive the girls to sailing," she said quietly.

Mocha shot up.

"Hey. I've got it covered." Ashley grinned, and tugged Mocha back down into the blankets next to her, breasts gently touching.

Mocha relaxed and blush-smiled. "Good morning."

"Good morning. You should stay and rest."

Mocha didn't resist. "Sailing wouldn't be much better for me than dune buggies."

"Didn't think so. I'll bring back tea and breakfast things." And she kissed Mocha's head again.

Mocha looked almost pained by the interaction and Ashley hoped she wasn't being too familiar. Doting was her default for the small fold of people she decided were her people.

And Mocha was starting to feel very much a part of that fold.

When Ashley entered the kitchen Cora was slathering a bagel with excessive cream cheese.

"Morning! Where's my cousin? Did you wear her out?"

Cora had no chill.

"You were right. We *really* liked the pie place."

Cora grinned, looking self-satisfied, and took a bite of her mostly-cream-cheese bagel.

Ashley was infinitely less suited to carting around a gaggle of giggly girls than Mocha seemed to be. Her annoyance with their snail's pace and excited squealing was immediate.

The sailing tickets had been crazy pricey per person

so Ashley had gotten out of it, and now that she had Mocha waiting in her bed she was especially glad. She snapped the obligatory photos of the boat, the girls posing against the boat and the water, the girls doing their extremely necessary King-of-the-World Titanic pose, and then waved them away for their two-hour cruise.

She found a drive-through coffee shop that thank God served espresso and got an Earl Grey tea latte for Mocha.

When she got back Mocha was still in bed and still naked.

She hid her smile as she proffered her tea and a bagel breakfast sandwich. Mocha sat up, blanket wrapped around her, and gratefully accepted both, watching Ashley down her coffee.

"How were you two and a half sips?"

"So good. Don't mock me over there, sipping tea and pretending to Miss-Americana-from-the-Sticks."

"Fair enough."

She couldn't help but notice that Mocha looked anxious, like she was torn between her desire to relax and enjoy breakfast in bed together and something else entirely.

"Something on your mind?"

"A lot of things," she admitted, sipping her tea harder and seeming to search for words. She finally settled on, "What do you want from me, Ashley?"

The wording caught her off guard.

"Um. To love you, I think."

That made Mocha cringe.

"And if that's too soon, to date you. I would love to date you and spend time with you and see what happens. And maybe do more of what we did last night. But I have no ulterior motives."

"No, I didn't think you did," Mocha clung to her cup of tea with both hands, like it was a lifeline. "Ashley, I am so scared to tell you this, but this part of me isn't something I've had any time or space to explore."

"I definitely got that part." She huddled in closer. "But the whole world doesn't have to know all at once. Your parents seem loving and supportive-ish?"

Mocha swallowed hard.

And then Ashley wondered if maybe they were the kind of loving and supportive parents who were only that way so long as you did what they wanted.

"I don't know if I'm ready, Ashley."

Oh.

Ashley's coffee suddenly hit a little different.

Fuck.

Fuck.

Fuck, fuck, fuck, fuck.

Panic, like she hadn't felt in ages, hit her.

Fuck, God, tell me I did not just open myself up again for her to be telling me this.

Ashley opened her mouth to respond and couldn't.

"It's that I'm living with my family right now. And they're paying for my school. For my dream. And they would really, really, not be able to handle or accept this."

"They wouldn't be able to handle or accept you

being who you are?" Ashley said numbly, mostly in hopes that Mocha would hear it the way she heard it. She knew full well not everyone could waltz into the out-and-proud daylight but she hoped, at least, that Mocha knew her parent's treatment wasn't healthy or loving.

She flinched a little. "No. I don't think they could."

"I'm sorry," she said, raggedly.

Mocha went on. "And I... I could try to see you in secret. But I'm so afraid it will all blow up. My parents would always be just next door. I would always wonder how long we could keep it up or keep it a secret, especially in Harper Port. And my cousin already suspects. And I... I don't know Ashley. I'm just freaking out."

Ashley's insides twisted instantly at the thought of sneaking around in hiding like her mom had to do for *years* just to be away from Dad's wrath.

She knew already she couldn't go back to that.

Mocha put her tea on the bedside table and huddled her knees to her chest. "Harper Port is my whole world, where all my family is. And I don't know that either of us would ever work another wedding there if it came out we were together. I'd be the tragic good-girl-led-astray and you'd be the lesbian-who-led-me-astray and no one wants that sort of scandal around their good reputable little country church wedding. And I'm not making the sort of money I could pay my way through school with yet. And not, especially, if I suddenly had to pay all my living expenses. I don't know how I'd juggle all that with still building my business. I don't know—"

Ashley took her hand.

She was feeling a little nauseated but tried to look reassuring.

"I am so sorry. I didn't think it was all so complicated." She was forced to admit, "I didn't... think."

Tears welled in Mocha's big green eyes and Ashley squeezed her hand tighter.

Ashley didn't mean for her voice to crack but it did. "I hope to God I didn't make you feel pressured to do anything you didn't want to do."

"No. No, no, no, I wanted to. So much. I just," Mocha looked away from her. "I'm afraid of what happens if we keep going."

"So, it can't happen again," Ashley said, mostly to herself.

Mocha rubbed her eyes. "I don't know, Ashley, I don't know. I feel sick to my stomach about it all."

"Hey," Ashley shoveled down her own emotions. "Don't. I don't want you to regret anything. It was so sweet and so perfect and it was a chance for you to be who you are. And I had one perfect night with you."

Mocha was weeping into the blanket now.

Jesus Christ, she hadn't been ready to have her freshly unfurling heart ripped out like this.

"Hey." She kissed her cheek. "It's okay. Mocha. I understand. I'm not mad. I just don't want you to regret it."

"I could never regret it," she wept.

"Okay. Good. Then. Let's not cry because it's over,

let's smile because it happened."

"Don't you Dr. Suess at me!"

"Okay. I won't if you stop crying. Because it's going to make me cry and," her voice frayed a little. "I can't take that right now."

Mocha reigned in her snuffles and lifted her flushed face.

Ashley feigned a little smile. "I don't want to think about the whole world right now, do you?"

Mocha shook her head.

"Good. I just want to have breakfast in bed with the stunning girl I had one of the sweetest nights of my life with. Is that okay?"

Mocha nodded.

"Good. Drink your tea."

Mocha took a compliant sip and Ashley tried to calm her pulse. She should have grabbed another espresso. She couldn't eat but she made a valiant effort.

Mocha dropped her bags in the entryway, dreamy, dazed, and depressed. Right now she just wanted to curl up in bed, cry, and dream of Ashley's hands on her over and over again.

But Mom accosted her in the hallway.

"MSU sent you a packet!"

"Oh. Great." She took it numbly, feeling like they

were papers that sealed her fate as a hostage.

Mom grinned like she held another secret.

"And. You and I are going shopping for interview clothes!"

"For what?"

"Daddy set you up for an interview with Warren & Warren on Friday."

"Dad. Did. *What?*"

Mom's eyes got a little large at the unexpected response.

"I thought he told you he was going to try to set you up with—"

"I didn't even apply."

"You know Daddy has connections."

Mocha's stomach, already queasy, gave a tilted lurch.

But seeing the surprise and hint of hurt in Mom's eyes she tried to put on some semblance of her usual self. "Thanks, Mom," she said numbly. "Maybe we can go shopping tomorrow?"

Mom relaxed and her voice was wistful, but it had the tiniest catch of something like venom in it. "My daughter, an MBA candidate. And a career woman."

"I'm gonna run out," she said quickly, knowing she would be too fitful to collapse into bed for her intended daydream and soul-searching session now.

"Where are you headed? When will you be back?"

"I don't know Mom it's just a walk, if I'm not back by nightfall send the National Guard."

Mom looked taken aback again and Mocha closed the door on her surprised face.

She rubbed her forehead.

She'd once heard of her aunts say to Mother, *Your Mocha is such a goody-two-shoes. Watch out for that one. Girls who don't go through a rebellious stage when they're little girls or teenagers go through one later in life.* She wondered if those words were echoing in Mom's head right now.

Her steps took her, unbidden, to the Flower Box.

Bundles of new flowers were in a display out front and she stepped inside, drawn by their smell.

Hayden-with-attitude was at the counter and Mocha rallied herself for the interaction, but then her old coworker Ross swooped out of nowhere and boomed, "Mocha!" a little too enthusiastically. He turned to the girl at the counter. "Hey, Kailey, why don't you go do the watering? In the back?"

The girl snapped her gum to assert dominance but she left.

He gave Mocha a little look. "This summer's kiddo crew is *not* working out. But you left shoes too big to fill. What can I do for you Mochi?"

"I need a gardenia bouquet."

"For a wedding?"

"No, um, for a gift."

She didn't send a card this time.

In the language of flowers, white gardenias meant *secret love*.

She didn't know if Ashley would be willing to carry on in secret. But maybe, if she was…

She listlessly poured through her organizer and binders that afternoon, made a few calls, and stared out of the window a lot. Ashley didn't seem to be home.

The next day there was a knock on the door mid-afternoon and Mocha raced to get it before her mom could.

She flung the door open and saw a van that wasn't a Flower Box van whizzing away. Something about this bouquet was different. Ashley had ordered it from the competing florist in town.

Her heart sank.

Striped carnations.

Striped carnations meant refusal.

The note was unsigned.

A clean break will be easier, baby girl. I am happy to see you as a friend. Thank you for the very sweet memory.

Mocha sat on the porch, unable to quite breathe. She didn't know what she'd been hoping for, but it wasn't *the door is closed*.

But Ashley didn't have anything to hide and it felt stupidly unfair to ask her to carry on in secret. Her family had lived in Michigan in secret for so many years to hide from her father. She was sure it got exhausting, living in hiding.

She was starting to learn a thing or two about it.

Mom appeared behind her.

"Oooh, who are those from?"

"Some guy," Mocha said bitterly.

CHAPTER 17

She couldn't stay away from Ashley. She tried, but she couldn't.

What are you doing today? She messaged. It was the text Ashley customarily sent.

Just editing. What's up?

I have a few clients to run by you, see if you want to set up a meeting with them.

Sure. Flower Box?

If Ashley's texts hadn't tended to run short and brisk before she'd have felt gut-punched.

Mocha stopped in surprise when she saw Ashley coming down the rainy sidewalk, huddled under a purple umbrella.

She... didn't look good.

She normally looked so put together and chill no matter the lounge clothes she was wearing or the disarray of her hair.

Today she walked a little dazedly through the glossy streets. Her hair was in a sad lopsided bun and her eyes brooding and dark.

She looked like every senior girl in college.

"'Morning," she said, casually.

"Hi," Mocha said quietly. She'd convinced herself that she was at home pining while Ashley just went on with her life. Now she didn't think so. "I'm finally to where I have people taking me seriously and wanting to book a year or more in advance. I have a few people trying to lock in next summer."

Ashley nodded and forced a smile. "That's so good, Mocha." She at least sounded genuine. "I'm gonna go get coffee before I fall over."

"Okay."

Mocha picked a table and went to order her tea.

When she got back to the table Ashley had three espressos lined up in front of her.

She took the first one like a shot.

"You look... tired."

"Thanks," she said dryly. Then, "I went to see Mom and Riley on Tuesday." The night she'd sent the carnations. "Had to be back Wednesday afternoon to meet with a couple." Yesterday.

"Aren't they close to Madison?"

Ashley nodded.

"Isn't that five hours from here?"

"Six if you need to Zen out, so you take the car ferry."

"That's a lot of driving."

"I needed a long ride," Ashley said, half-draining her second espresso. Then, as if trying to be more lighthearted, "We grew up begging my mom to take the car ferry so I do it at least once a year."

"That sounds like fun," Mocha said weakly.

Silence lapsed between them. Pained silence.

"I wanted to see if you wanted me to refer you to these two," Mocha pushed a couple's profile towards Ashley. "Their photography budget is a little limited."

"I'm just a little tiny bit out of their price range for six hours. But. This early on, if they wanted to book me, I'd break up the payment plan and throw in an engagement shoot for free."

"I'll let them know." She scribbled down a note.

She wished she didn't feel like this was all a stiff business meeting.

She wanted to blurt to Ashley that her father had set up an internship interview for her tomorrow, without her permission, but she wondered if that would sound whiney and privileged. She wanted to tell her that she felt like her brides did when the world was spinning out of control and no one was interested in what you thought or felt.

She wanted it to not feel like Saugatuck had never happened.

In a rush of desperation she blurted, "By the way, if you still need a model for your boudoir photos, I'll do it."

Ashley stared at her, espresso frozen halfway to her mouth. "I don't think your parents would like that."

Mocha felt like a little girl who wasn't being taken seriously. She hated the feeling.

"Well, you'd only show prospective clients, right?"

"And put them on my website."

"Oh."

"I guess I could use ones that don't show your face."

Her heart lifted at the proposition.

Ashley stared into her cup for a minute before polishing it off. "I don't know."

"Look," Mocha said, earnestly. "I don't want things to be weird between us. I still want to be around you. I still want things to be like they were before."

Ashley nodded, and again, she looked like an adult just entertaining the ideas of a child, and it made Mocha fume inside.

But she did ask, "What are you doing tomorrow afternoon?"

Her interview was in the morning.

"I'm free after 12."

Ashley didn't look at her when she said, "Then come on over. I'll text you a list of things to bring."

"It's an incredible opportunity," the interviewer said, shuffling around papers. "We have about a week and a half of interviews left before we start making decisions."

Mocha thanked him and walked stiffly to her car in her stiff suit-and-skirt. If her parents only knew where she was headed after the interview.

Ashley had sent a text the night before.

-My friend at Curls and Pearls will do your hair and makeup for free, she owes me a favor. Stop by at 12:15

-Bring your favorite underwear/intimates (at least 3-4 looks) and we can work with those. Robes, corsets, a sweater or cardigan, stockings, and sports jerseys are fun too if you have any.

-Bring any favorite jewelry or accessories. I have a wedding veil, hair flowers, pearls.

-Bring at least one pair of heels.

-Don't get drunk off your ass, I will have *light* drinks

Mocha blushed at the last bullet. Ashley could read her mind. She'd wondered all morning whether getting sloshed would loosen her inhibitions. If it had been just any boudoir shoot she would have been intimidated, but Ashley in the mix excited and terrified her.

She'd piled the items into a giant beach tote and snuck it into her car before the interview. She'd also worn a yellow sundress under her shirt and skirt and parked at the local park to wriggle out of the stiff outfit—much to the gaping awe of a few passing teenagers.

When she walked through the door at Curls and Pearls a redheaded girl scurried over. "Are you Ashley's girlfriend?"

Mocha was stricken. "Ashley's…"

"Or sorry. *Friend.*" She winked. "Ashley thinks the world of you. Said I have to take very good care of you. Made that same exact adorable I-don't-know-what-you're-talking-about look when I asked how *close* of a friend."

The girl waved Mocha to a chair in the rear corner of the salon and Mocha did a quick visual check of the clientele. She recognized one of the women from Mom's Weekday Social club that Dad not-so-playfully called a cult. But she was absorbed in chatting with her hairdresser and didn't see Mocha, and luckily, didn't hear the redheaded stylist chattering away.

"How long have you known Ashley?"

"She's been my neighbor for three years. We only met this summer."

"Oh wow, you were missing out! She and Tess threw the best parties. She's the best kind of friend. I owe her *way* more favors than this one, but this is the only one she's ever called in."

She pumped the chair aggressively to height and waved Mocha into it.

The session flew by and before Mocha knew it her hair was piled in a luxurious, romantic updo. Her rosy face of makeup was just natural enough that she wasn't afraid to run into any acquaintances, just glamorous enough that she was afraid they might ask what fancy event she was running off to.

She crept quickly out of the salon, hoping Mom's friend didn't glance up and recognize her.

She parked around the block from Ashley's and her knock on the purple door sounded a little shaky.

Ashley opened, looking a little less tortured than yesterday, but maybe a little *too* put together. Professional.

"You look lovely. I have Moscato or I have champagne."

"I'll take champagne, please," she said, ignoring how the compliment rattled her. Champagne gave her a buzz faster. Tofu appeared and twirled around Mocha's ankles while Ashley popped the bottle and poured the sparkling liquid into a flute.

She poured orange juice into a flute for herself, just orange juice, and passed the champagne to Mocha, lifting her glass for a toast.

"What are we toasting to?"

"How about that fabulous sundress?" But she said it in a sterile way, almost casually.

They sipped.

And then Ashley was back to business. "I set up in

the guest room, away from your parent's windows." She led the way and the room was arranged in true studio style, with the light stand and the umbrella and the flash and the fan and the video light panel and other things Mocha didn't know the name or function of.

"Can I see the outfits you brought?"

Mocha lowered the tote bag to the floor and backed away like it held a bomb. Ashley rifled through her naughtiest underthings like it was nothing.

"Oh, I love the hell out of this," she said, tugging out a Spartans baseball jersey. "We'll pair it with this," she said, lifting out a black bra and panties.

She laid the outfit aside, picked a pink bra-panty set, a lilac bra-panty set, and a cardigan, and…

"Whoa." She extracted a light blue corset.

"It was for a Halloween costume. I was Alice in Wonderland."

"I'm sure you were," she looked like she was trying to stifle a *look*. "We're definitely using *that*." She tugged loose lacy stockings to go with it. Then she set aside the two pairs of heels Mocha had brought along, one lilac and one pink. She didn't have any black heels and had been too paralyzed to ask Mom about borrowing any of hers.

Ashley stood and started snapping photos of Mocha as she was, standing blankly in the middle of the floor. "You look amazing. Drape yourself in that chair and sip your champagne?"

Mocha did so and Ashley continued snapping as though the shoot had already started. "I like the pair of Converse you're wearing now for when we do the baseball jersey. Drape your legs over the arm of the chair?"

She dangled her legs and took another swig of champagne.

"Cute. You're the prettiest girl I've shot today."

"Ha," she snorted. "Hahahaha."

"Do that again?"

"Do what again?"

"Give me that face you make when you're annoyed at me."

"*What* face?"

CHAPTER 18

Ashley grinned at her. "That one." And she snapped several shots of it. Then she lowered her camera. "I'll leave you to get changed into whatever outfit you like first—"

"Oh," Mocha said, falteringly. "I wore my favorite underwear set under this. If that's too many looks…"

"No, that's perfect," Ashley said. "I can leave you—"

But Mocha, maybe motivated by the champagne, had stood and was already lifting her sundress up and over her head. She let it fall to the floor.

Her favorite underwear set had been one of the ones that Ashley had gotten in her mailbox back in May, the teal bra and panties.

Ashley cleared her throat. "Great. Let's get started.

I'm gonna have you throw on some pearls with that. And then I'm going to have you look out the window and keep drinking that champagne."

She had Mocha look out the window, and then perch on the window seat, and then grabbed a cup that was sitting on a warmer that Mocha hadn't noticed before, and had her hold it and swig from it. It was chamomile tea.

"Your hands are perfect," Ashley said.

She had no idea what she was doing with her hands but tried to keep it up.

"These are great. Get into the jersey and the black bra and panties. Start with the Converse on."

And Ashley left her alone in the room and Mocha felt the loss of her company.

The afternoon continued with that crisp, professional, but playful ease.

She had Mocha sit on a stool, huddle up in blankets, and put on her cardigan over her lilac bra and panties.

"Stick your head out towards me, using your neck. Like a turkey." Mocha found herself giggling throughout at Ashley's colorful explanations of poses and facial expressions.

"What actress would make you swoon? Of course. Okay. Well, smile like Scar Jo just walked in here. Never mind. If you ever meet Scar Jo please don't make that face."

She next arranged a bundle of flowers on the bed and nestled Mocha in the middle of them.

"I feel like I'm on a funeral pyre."

"There will be no fire. You and your fucking fire."

Throughout, Ashley made her feel beautiful, but in a way she had never felt beautiful before.

She marveled at how comfortable she was, especially when she wriggled into the corset and stockings and heels to pose on the hallway stairs.

Ashley looked like she was trying a little too hard to keep her face impassive at the sight of Mocha in the corset.

"How opposed would you be to a blindfold?"

"A what now?" Mocha blanched.

"That outfit with you kneeling on the floor and a blindfold. The 50 Shades stuff is very in. Weirdly enough, especially here."

"I," she swallowed. "Think I would be okay with it."

And Ashley produced a blindfold from her props like it was a Kleenex or any other old item.

She delicately fastened it over Mocha's eyes, without mussing her updo.

"Okay. Perfect. Kneel again."

She trembled ever so faintly while Ashley coached her, blinded, through various poses.

"And if you're comfortable we'll try something. I think we're good on your updo. Do you mind if I let it down?"

"Not at all." She didn't exactly want to waltz back home in it anyway.

Ashley skillfully tugged a few pins loose and the hair came tumbling down. Mocha could feel it rather than see, still blindfolded.

"Okay," Ashley lifted her up and guided her to sit on the bed. "If you're comfortable, I'm going to take off your corset. You're going to pull your knees against your chest to hide your breasts. And then you're going to arrange your hair to obscure one breast keeping the other covered with your knee folded against your chest. Make sense?"

Mocha hoped Ashley couldn't perceive her shakiness.

"Okay," she agreed.

Ashley began to unhook her corset from behind. When it fell away from her Mocha pulled her knees to her chest.

"Perfect. Now…" Mocha remembered the instructions. She lowered her left knee and arranged her honey-colored hair over her breast.

"Gorgeous. Perfect."

Ashley hopped off the bed and Mocha could hear the camera shutter. She instructed Mocha to cross her legs, uncross them, drape them.

"I'm going to put some flowers in your hair and take off the blindfold." And she did so very gently, the warm light in the room and the sensation of Ashley's closeness filling Mocha's senses again.

Ashley returned to photographing and paused to check what she'd captured so far. "These are fucking gorgeous."

Mocha, even blindfold-free, was more aroused than she meant to be.

"You could cup your right breast with your hand and lower your knee."

She tremblingly did so, slowly lowering her leg.

"Stunning. Okay. And finally. *If* you're comfortable, we're going to do a tasteful nude with a wedding veil. Is that okay?"

Mocha didn't know how much more heat she could take, but she nodded. Ashley knelt beside her and fastened the veil into her loose hair, so delicately she hardly felt it. Then she spread the veil around her half-naked body.

"Should I..." Mocha faltered. "Take off the panties?"

"If you want to, a clean nude outline could be really pretty," Ashley's voice sounded a little tight. "I'd arrange you so that everything would be hidden. Would that be okay?"

"It would be."

Before Ashley could turn around she hobbled to her feet, hair and veil just barely concealing her body, and faced away from Ashley to take her panties off, knowing full well that if Ashley was still looking she'd see her bottom quite clearly.

When she turned back she could see Ashley taking a second to compose herself.

"Perfect. Let me set you on the stool."

She handled Mocha like she was made of glass. "Okay." Her voice had lost its buoyancy. "We're going to bend your knees and you're going to wrap this arm across your breasts. Just perfect."

She stepped back and took a long minute to get her camera and the lighting to the settings she wanted.

"Just keep being yourself."

And she seemed very focused on what she was capturing. She made Mocha gather the lace around herself in various ways, concealing various parts with tendrils of hair, or a hand, or a swath of lacy cloth.

And then she finally lowered her camera and said, "I think we're about done."

Disappointed flooded Mocha's senses.

Her bare nipples were pert and she hoped she wasn't getting wet, sitting here naked on the stool.

She wanted nothing more in the world than for Ashley to jump her just then, but she just unfastened her camera lens.

"I'll leave you to get dressed and packed up," she said crisply. Professionally. Of course, Mocha wouldn't have expected anything else.

Her dress back on and her things back in her beach tote, she crept into the living room where Ashley was looking through her camera.

"These are so, so good," she smiled, without looking up at Mocha as she approached. "Thank you so much. I'll show you before I use anything."

"Since I'm not driving after this," she ventured shyly. "I wouldn't resist another glass of champagne."

"And since I'm no longer on the clock, I think I'll have one too."

They poured two more sparkling glasses and hovered inside the kitchen, sipping silently.

Mocha tried, so hard, to sound casual. "For the Lance wedding, I got a hotel room since it's so far out of town and we'll be done so late. It has two beds. I could add you to the room?"

Ashley looked down, and Mocha instantly regretted it.

"I'm not trying to lead you on," she blurted. "Or anything. I just know that I... hate not being near you."

Ashley took a long swig of her champagne.

And then said, numbly, "Forward me the bill and I'll Venmo you for half."

The minute Mocha was out the front door Ashley texted her sister furiously.

Everything is such a fucking mess.

Oh, God. Did something happen?

She came over today. For a boudoir shoot.

Like the kind where you get naked?

They are sensual photos, yes.

She drained her champagne and then resumed texting.

It's like I said. It's complicated with her family. And I could never live in hiding again. But I legit can't stop thinking about her. I haven't felt this way since Tess.

Her phone lit up with a call. It was Riley. Apparently, texting wasn't doing it. She reluctantly answered and Riley skipped over greetings.
"You can't compare everything to Tess."
The words hit like a brick.
"I'm not."
"You are, Ash. I love you and I love Tess. And I know you'll always love her too. But this isn't about Tess. It's about you and somebody new. So let's focus on that."
Ashley raked a hand through her hair and tried to think straight. She had called Riley crying after each of the dates she had been on the last two years and after her holiday party hookup. The girl at Christmas had felt like such a betrayal because she had enjoyed it too much. And the girl wasn't anything like Tess at all. Cropped short hair, boyish clothing, blue eyes, a gamer type, a nerd, but so witty, so adorable, so delightful to touch.
She'd felt the flood of guilt after, for feeling so good with someone so unlike the love of her life.
Mocha was nothing like Tess either. Outdoorsy Tess with her litany of mountain and forest and moon-themed tattoos, dragging Ashley on infinitely many hikes. Tess, whose steady brown gaze was anything but wide and innocent, who had seen some things and been through some things. Tess with all her frilly fancy coffee.
They'd each been the other's first. It felt all wrong that Tess had never slept with anyone but her, and

Ashley had been with a handful of women now.

But what she didn't know how to articulate to Riley, what felt callous to say, was that Tess's ghost wasn't the problem anymore.

"So, what do I do? Throw caution to the wind and date her in secret and sneak around like teenaged girls? In the end, it's going to blow up and I don't know that we'll make it to the other side."

"You could give it time."

She flopped into her chair and unintentionally stared at Mocha's house, even though the afternoon sun would block her view of anything from the windows. But Mocha wasn't inside, she was on the porch. She was scribbling a bit solemnly in one of her notebooks.

Ashley stood and went back to the kitchen.

Don't tell anybody our address, she'd had to say to friends when they wrote letters throughout childhood. And they rarely let it be known that they were home in Wisconsin in the summer because the word could get back to Dad. *Hide, hide, hide,* it had been a suffocating way to do a childhood. Ashley couldn't imagine doing it as an adult.

But then, those secret summers had been the best of her life. She couldn't tell her friends where they were staying, or that they were in town long-term, but she and Riley got to run wild at Grandma's and pick flowers and swim in the lake all day and eat Grandma's cooking.

Sixth grade was the year Mom left Dad, and that year her favorite book was *Tuck Everlasting.* She re-

read it every summer. She was re-reading it the day she met Tess. In her head, she always substituted Jesse Tuck for an older girl. She was at her favorite part, the part when Winnie takes her fate into her own hands and sneaks out to save the Tuck family. That was when she noticed a girl.

The girl was walking up the path with a fishing pole, looking a little lost, and the girl was Tess.

Riley said what Ashley now knew. "Tess would want you to love, Ashley."

She rubbed her eyes and tried to breathe.

She caught a glimpse of her shoulder tattoos in the mirror and stared at the entangled stems. She'd finally hit the culmination of her grief. She'd never be able to disentangle herself from Tess. That didn't necessarily mean she could never experience any other entanglements of the heart again.

But now…

She admitted the root of this new ache. "I think the problem is I know that now. I know that I'm allowed to get on with my life. But I feel like, now that I feel ready to… I'm up against a brick wall."

"Then maybe it's not Mocha. Maybe it's somebody else. But you've already won half the battle, Ashley. You're ready to live again."

CHAPTER 19

The Evans-Lance wedding had a *Phantom of the Opera* meets *Beauty and the Beast* theme with romantic and dramatic flair, and already the pending drama felt high.

The bridesmaids were clustered together before getting-ready photos while the bride was out getting her hair done. They acted like Ashley didn't exist and chattered while she took photos of their matching sapphire blue robes and monogrammed makeup bags.

"How bad do you think today is going to be?"

"Maybe she'll be chill."

The bride's sister snorted. "They spent $28,000 on this. She made us all learn calligraphy to hand-letter the invitations. There will be no chill."

"I still have burns on my hands from those hot wax

seals."

Ashley could feel her soul shriveling. She'd had very few bridezillas. Momzillas, jealous wedding parties, and warring family members were usually the source of wedding drama. She hoped today wouldn't break her good luck streak.

"She quit her job to work on the wedding full-time you know," said the sister, sipping her mimosa.

The bridesmaids all nodded dazedly. They already knew. Oh, Lordy Lord.

The bride had given the bridesmaids silver hand mirrors with a very *Beauty and the Beast* feel and Ashley lined them up to get a cool flower-reflection effect.

Then the door bust open.

Bea Evans sailed in wearing her sapphire lace-trimmed robe, with Mocha and the mother of the bride following. Ashley felt instant confusion because Beatrice seemed sweet as pie, just as chill as she'd been in their pre-wedding meeting. She squealed and all the girls did too and got up to hug her and squeal about her hair and makeup.

They stayed far away from the bride's mother.

"Oh good!" The mother bellowed. "The photographer. I need to have a word with you."

Mocha began to mouth words to her but she didn't have time to catch them. It looked a little like, *If you need help, scream.*

Ashley followed the woman into the hall where she turned and looked at Ashley like she was sizing her up. She'd faced off with her fair share of moms so she tried to strike the delicate balance of laid-back but also don't-fuck-with-me.

"My husband and I are footing the entire bill for this. Including *yours.*"

"Yes, ma'am," Ashley said, and the woman looked a little stiffly pleased to be acknowledged for the *ma'am* that she was.

"I quit my job for this. Even with a wedding planner, it was a full-time job to put this occasion together."

Holy... moly...

"I see."

"So, because of that. I have one request for you. One only."

"Yes, ma'am?"

"You will not be taking *any* photos of the groom's family."

"I'm sorry, what?"

"The groom's mother, his three sisters, and his deadbeat stepfather. I don't want any of them in any single one of *our* pictures."

The fuck?

"I'm sorry, I would absolutely have to check with the bride and the groom about that first."

"But *we* are paying your—"

"I understand that, but contractually I am obligated to the couple's vision. And they definitely requested specific photos with the groom and his family members."

And they were doing a mother-son dance.

And the groom's youngest sister was the flower girl! Was she supposed to just *not* photograph the flower girl?? She tried to keep her absolute appall in check.

"I will chat with the bride and groom about your request. *Contractually,* that is what I would have to do."

The woman visibly fumed. "If they aren't paying for any part of this wedding I don't see why they should be represented in *our* family heirlooms!"

Ashley thought she'd overheard that they put on a lovely rehearsal dinner the evening before.

The woman barreled on. "And since *I* am the one footing your bill—"

If she wasn't going to stop…"Technically. Your husband is the one who wrote me the check." She said it as non-confrontationally as possible.

The woman paused, looking like a splotched piglet. "We are *husband* and *wife*—"

"But only his name was on the check."

Mom finally realized that Ashley was not the one to bully. She was speechless and Ashley filled the gap. "I'll check with your husband and the bride and groom—"

"No. That won't be necessary." She looked like she could spit flames. "I understand perfectly. I hope you're happy to forego a tip."

"I am the owner of my company, so general etiquette dictates it's not necessary to tip." She smiled politely.

And the woman finally stormed back into the getting-ready room.

The bride was all aglow until her mother stepped into the room and Mocha saw it instantly.

"Mrs. Evans I actually need your final approval on

some finishing touches to the centerpieces."

She straightened importantly. "Of course."

Mocha led her out giving Ashley a brief little look. "We'll be back before the bride gets into her dress!"

The instant the door closed behind them the party relaxed a little.

"Is your robe monogrammed on the back?" Ashley said, by way of distraction. Bea grinned.

"It is!" She spun in her chair so Ashley could see the *Mrs. Lance* in big swirly white letters.

"I need a shot of that. You should run to the window and throw open the curtains. You're getting married today!"

The bride's grin was back, and Ashley got some lovely sunlit photos. The girls popped champagne for more mimosas and posed with their etched champagne flutes. Then Ashley settled in for photos of them getting their makeup done and of the bride putting on her sapphire heels.

True to her word, Mocha kept the mother of the bride busy until just before it was time to get into the dress.

Luckily then there was something to keep her busy with. Ashley snapped photos while the woman meticulously fastened every single dress button.

The whole rest of the day was a juggling act of keeping Mrs. Evans from raining on everyone's parade, but especially her daughter's. The couple did a first look, which worked beautifully for getting them some alone time. Ashley and Mocha finally got a quiet moment together driving back from the first-look spot to the ceremony spot.

"You won't believe what the mother of the bride asked me."

Mocha did *not* believe it.

"Are you fucking serious?"

Ashley nodded.

"Are you fucking kidding me? This rabid monster of a woman has done nothing but try to make this beautiful day all about her miserable self."

Ashley snorted. "A little worked up about this."

"I *am!* I'm sorry but I can't handle attention whores at weddings."

"Whoa. Do you kiss your mother what that mouth?"

"No. I've only kissed you with it."

Ashley wasn't used to being the one caught off guard.

Mocha turned back to her clipboard. "The plan is to knock out family photos before the ceremony, thank God, because we need to get the bridal party away from that troll during cocktail hour."

"Good plan."

The juggling act continued. Mocha cornered the DJ before the reception to give him a pre-approved list of speakers for speeches, which Mrs. Evans was very much so not on. Ashley made sure to be very much in the woman's line of sight for the father-daughter dance and very much out of her sight while photographing the mother-son dance. Luckily, Mocha distracted her with highly important questions about the twinkle lights on the favor table, so the woman didn't just stand on the fringe of the dance floor and glare.

Ashley loved every second of watching Mocha do what she did best.

The day was all chandeliers, roses in gold trumpets, stained glass, and twinkle-lit trees and fountains. The photos Ashley captured were as deliciously angsty-romantic as you could get, and most definitely included the groom's smiling family.

And by sheer force of will, they made it to the end of the day without a major mom incident.

When the couple ran off to their getaway carriage amid sparkler light and the guests began to disperse, Ashley wanted to collapse immediately. She drifted to a fountain reflecting all the twinkle lights in the trees and dropped onto the bench facing it.

Mocha approached and she pretended not to be highly aware of it.

"Holy 21,000 steps," she muttered glancing at her smart watch as Mocha perched on the bench next to her. She tried to ignore how romantic it all was, the smell of the night air and the sparkling trees and the fountain. "21k. That's almost as much as Mrs. Evans supposedly spent on this wedding."

"Short *only* seven thousand."

"I hope you got a slice of that. You really should start charging what you're worth."

"I'm getting there." She waved around at the general twinkle-lit splendor. "Building that portfolio."

"Well, this is one for the books. And speaking of portfolios. I finished editing the boudoir photos." She tried to say it impassively. "I'll show you tonight if you're not too wiped out."

The makeup on Mocha's face concealed any flush that might have sprung up there.

The hotel room was cozy, with maritime themed everything. Mocha dropped her bag and Ashley put her duffel on one of the beds. "I'm going to crawl out of these clothes." And to Mocha's disappointment, she went into the bathroom to do so.

Mocha changed quickly herself, squirming into a tie-dye t-shirt and shorts.

When Ashley returned she looked highly snuggle-able in a tank top and shorts.

Ashley flopped onto the couch and Mocha joined her, sitting close.

"So here," Ashley flipped her MacBook open, "are the ones I'd like to use in my portfolio."

Mocha stared. She hardly recognized the woman in the photos as herself. Each selection concealed her identity and her privacy with expert subtlety. Chest-down or face turned away, hair cloaking her face, shadow concealing her face, or only her lips down.

"Are all those okay?"

"Oh yes. They're so beautiful."

"So those are the ones I will use. But these are my favorites."

The first of Ashley's favorites showed Mocha with flowers caught in her hair. It was followed by her laughing in her baseball jersey, then tangled in the wedding veil. Then, she was kneeling with the blindfold, biting her lip, face upturned. In the final favorite, she gave Ashley her "annoyed face" in just her sundress, cradling the glass of champagne.

"Ashley these are beautiful. You have… *so* much talent."

"You supplied all the beauty."

The tension fluttered between them like a moth, and when Ashley didn't look at her, Mocha found her boldness again.

"Why don't we share a bed?"

"Mocha." She said it chidingly.

"I'm sorry. I know. I'm sorry."

Ashley did face her then. She took her hands. "Trust me. Sneaking around will implode. Your parents live next door to me. We work in all the same circles. And I don't want to ruin your life."

"I know," she said, numbly, looking down at the obnoxious pattern of her shirt.

"And I don't want just flings with you."

"I don't want that either."

Ashley laughed lightly. "I don't think you know what you want, sweetheart."

She didn't deny that. She knew what she secretly wanted, but what she wanted for her whole life was another story.

Ashley took a shuddering breath. "If we share the bed, we're only going to sleep."

"Okay." She kept staring at her pants. "Maybe kiss?"

Mocha could *feel* her quail a little. "You're making this so difficult."

"I'm sorry. Before you, I was the queen of clean breaks. I cut all my ex-boyfriends off cold turkey."

"Savage." Ashley scoffed. "Let's go to bed."

Mocha turned down the covers and Ashley flicked off all the lights except for the dim lamp on her side of the bed.

They snuggled in together under the sheets and when the scent of Ashley's hair and soft skin hit her all she could feel was absolute blissful content.

At first, Ashley only put a hand on her waist and rubbed her thumb gently there. Then Mocha shifted and inched closer.

She didn't know who kissed who first, but their lips met all in a rush.

They made out for what felt like hours, the caresses tender and hot and fervid. Somehow, each wriggled out of their pants and stroked each other through panties, soft and sensual and then hot and heavy.

Mocha didn't know she could feel this attached to another person, this in tune with someone. It was so wild and new and wonderful and sweet and…

"I really do adore you," Mocha whispered in a moment of vulnerable impulse, cradling Ashley's face in both hands and savoring a long, tender kiss.

When she ended the kiss, Ashley was trembling.

And she was crying.

"I can't do this. I just can't."

Alarmed, Mocha sat up and flicked on the light on her side of the bed. Tears were streaming down Ashley's face. She sat up and faced away from Mocha. "I have been in a lot of pain for a very long time and I don't think I can take anymore, Mocha."

And she started sobbing. Full body-wracking sobs.

Mocha was stunned. And she felt like a despicable human. "Ashley. I am so sorry."

"My heart. Just. Can't. Take. Anymore."

She'd thought Ashley had sent those carnations to protect *her*. She'd thought her determination not to sneak around was all for her own sake. "I was being selfish," she whispered, putting a hand on each arm, trying to gather her close, trying to comfort her.

She'd thought she was the only one with everything at stake.

"I'm feeling things I didn't think I could feel again," Ashley wept. "And if I keep touching you and having these moments with you, I know I'm going to want more. And if that's never going to happen, I can't torture myself with hoping."

"I really didn't mean to hurt you, Ashley. I'll sleep in the other bed."

"No." Ashley put a staying arm on her hand. "Listen, Mocha, I love every second spent with you. But I can't touch you, not like that, and I can't kiss you. Not right now."

The next morning Ashley squeezed her hand wordlessly in the parking lot before driving home, and Mocha drove dazedly into town. She didn't feel like the Flower Box because she knew full well she wouldn't be able to get her mind off Ashley there, but she couldn't face the smothering energy of her home and her parents just yet either.

She ended up at the bagel shop and found a table to pore over her binders and paperwork. She added the testimonial from the barn wedding to her website, adding a snapshot of the happy couple.

When she finally stumbled through her parent's front door both Dad and Mom were hovering in the front of the house.

"Mocha!" Dad barked. "Where *were* you?"

She stopped. She tried to keep the usual level of sweetness in her voice. "Working?"

"We didn't know you had an event today."

"A wedding. Yesterday. I told you I got a hotel."

"We thought you'd be back this morning," Mom said, accusatorily.

She almost said, *"You thought wrong,"* but reigned in her inner teenage girl who was sick and tired of this shit.

"I assume you haven't been checking your messages?"

She hadn't. She reached into her pocket for her

phone and saw it had about a dozen missed calls and six messages.

Almost all the calls were from her parents, but one was from a number she didn't recognize.

"Sorry," she said, slipping her phone back into her pocket. "I just got busy."

But neither of them looked satisfied. "Well, *are* you going to check your messages?"

Finally, the meaning of this ambush sank in.

If Warren & Warren was offering her a job, Dad was probably the first to know.

She wouldn't give them the satisfaction of checking in front of their faces. "I'll go to my room and catch up on everything right now."

And without giving them a second to protest she ran up the stairs and slammed the door behind her.

She listened to the voicemail in numb expectation.

"We would like to offer you the opportunity to intern with us…"

She could've cried, and then felt like a spoiled brat for wanting to. Not everyone could have Daddy run out and arrange a prestigious internship.

She huddled up under her quilt and went to sleep.

When sunset fell and there was a knock on the door she wiped away the quiet tears she'd been crying.

"Come in."

It was Mom.

"Well? Did you hear from Warren & Warren?"

"I did," she said numbly.

"And?"

"I got the business internship."

"Oh, Mocha!" Mom pretended to be surprised and sat on the edge of the bed. "This will be so good."

"And difficult to maintain while I'm in school."

Mom was unfazed. "Well Warner Warren is a friend of Daddy's, of course, so they're going to be flexible with your school schedule. And you'll be set with an internship like this. You won't need your wedding planner jobs anymore."

Mocha rubbed her eyes. "So I got the job because of who my father is and I'll get special treatment because of who my father is."

She could feel rather than see Mom's shock. "Mocha." Her voice was firm. "You know most kids would be grateful. And most people *with* an MBA would take this opportunity."

"You're right," she said. "Thanks. I'm tired. I'm just going to stay holed up in here tonight."

When Mom left Mocha let herself properly cry. She could still faintly smell Ashley on her skin, in her hair.

Masturbation sounded better than pure misery, so she rolled onto her back and began stroking herself, trying to mentally recreate Saugatuck. If nothing else, there was that one perfect night.

She was just getting into a rhythm, just starting to mentally create the rainy perfection and the feel of Ashley's hands on her—when there was *more* pounding on the door.

"Honey, can I have your laundry?"

She whisked her hand out of panties and lost it.

"I am a grown-ass woman and I can do my own

laundry, Mother! How do you think I had clean clothes for four years?!"

Stunned silence came from the other side of the door.

And then, finally, Mom's footsteps retreated quietly.

And it finally clicked for Mocha.

She needed to raise her prices. She needed to move out. She needed to fucking grow up.

CHAPTER 20

The weekend of Cora's August wedding dawned sunny and bright.

She'd be seeing Ashley tonight, and maybe, now that she was decided about moving out of her parent's home, there was a small hope. She hadn't told anyone about her decision yet. She'd asked the Warrens for a week to think about the opportunity, and they'd sounded surprised, but they assented. Then she shoved it to the very back of her mind.

The extravagant affair that was Cora and Mason's wedding would take place on a gigantic mansion estate, rented out entirely by Cora's father, and Mocha pulled up feeling a new rush of power. She had to corner Ashley and tell her that she'd decided to move out at least, and maybe then…

No, she knew she shouldn't give Ashley that hope, not yet. She knew she still wouldn't be any less beholden to what her parents thought of her, especially if Dad was still paying for school.

There had to be something. Some way this could all work.

Because she was trembling with anticipation at the mere prospect of seeing Ashley tonight at the rehearsal dinner.

She directed the venue staff through the setup plan and then directed the bridesmaids to properly set up the table décor, and that was just for the rehearsal dinner hall. Then it was time to decorate the room where the bridesmaids would be getting ready in the morning, set up the library where the groomsmen were getting ready, and roll out the tables for the actual reception space.

To anyone else, it would have looked like a frenzy of absolute chaos, but Mocha felt very much in her zone, and it at least helped the time pass.

When she saw the time was 3:00 she thought, *Rehearsal and then Ashley will be here,* instead of *Rehearsal and then Rehearsal Dinner.*

Rehearsal went off without a hitch and with many giggles, Cora and Mason beaming into each other's eyes. Cora's dad was officiating because he had gone to seminary before Cora's mom assured him she would never marry a pastor. So he'd gone into luxury real estate instead.

Mocha was proud of the magic she'd created in the banquet hall where the rehearsal dinner was served.

The table settings were white and gold with a long runner of eucalyptus and blush roses, just an early hint of tomorrow night's blush-and-burgundy magic. Her aunt looked around a little askance because the original talks for the rehearsal dinner had been very pink-silver-blue centric, but she seemed to finally satisfy herself that at least her own wedding color was represented.

And then finally, there was Ashley.

She appeared as quietly as she always did, like she'd always been there. She was breathtaking in a violet dress.

Mocha knew this level of desire to be close to her wasn't ordinary. Anything she'd ever felt before paled in comparison to this desire to catch Ashley's eyes and make her smile.

But Ashley was very much ready for work.

She photographed the details and photographed the guests as they milled about and got cocktails and admired the table settings and chandeliers and the golden candlesticks Cora had decided on last minute.

Even though they'd only invited family and the bridal party to the rehearsal dinner, family was a good bulk of the wedding guest list, so the hall buzzed with loud activity.

Mocha had just finished asking for a tall glass of water at the bar when Ashley appeared at her side unexpectedly, and the composure she'd held onto so hard seeped away.

She blurted, "Ash, you look stunning."

"Thank you," Ashley looked taken aback, such a

rare look on her face that Mocha couldn't help but savor it.

"You look enchanting. But you always do." Ashley glanced around as if to make sure no one was close enough to hear the exchange. "I thought I'd get the rundown just to know the flow of the night. I'm guessing there will be speeches?"

Just then Mocha's parents walked in and Mocha felt a strange lurch. She'd known they'd be here, of course, but for them to walk into her world at this split second, now that she was in Ashley's orbit, was off-putting.

"Yes," Mocha tried to turn her attention back to Ashley. "And a slideshow of the happy couple, at my aunt's insistence. One of the very few battles we let her win. Some of your engagement party photos are definitely in there. And then they're giving gifts to the bridal party to wrap up the night, thanking everybody, and we're out."

Her parents spotted her and waved and she waved stiffly back. Ashley turned and saw who she was waving to. She waved at Mocha's mom, who returned warmly.

"Is that your dad?" Ashley asked. "I guess I've never seen him up-close before."

"Mm-hmm." Mocha gulped her water.

"Awww. He looks like he's going to sell me life insurance."

Mocha almost spit the water back out.

Cora and Mason were posing under an arch of flowers for a selfie and Ashley blitzed off to capture the moment. Mocha knew the evening would keep them apart but that didn't stop her eyes from following her. Ashley constantly caught moments of beauty that Mocha wouldn't have otherwise noticed. Her gift for navigating rooms invisibly was surprising for someone so striking. But whenever she emerged from the shadows to interact or assist or recommend people arrange themselves a certain way, she was always inviting, warm, and charming. Mocha couldn't help but love watching her capture and create magic in the background.

Cora ambushed Mocha, already holding a glass of white wine. "It's so beautiful Mochi." She stood next to her to take in the room—and Ashley. "I'm so happy I have two of the very best wedding vendors in Michigan. You two really are a dream team."

"You can stop. I'm not going to run away with the photographer."

"Well, that's a shame. I saw the way you looked at her the whole Saugatuck weekend." She tapped Mocha's nose. "And I see the way she looks at *you* when she thinks no one is watching."

That thought made Mocha ache more than she wanted.

"Cora. This weekend is about you. Let's focus on you."

"Yes, but it's a wedding weekend! Mason and I made a bingo card. There's a whole line for wedding flings and flirtations."

Mocha looked quickly around to make sure her parents were nowhere nearby. Then she tried to keep her voice light, playfully interrogative, but it came out more weak than anything. "It's all fun and well to joke but would you really love and accept me if I fell in love with a woman? Or would I just always be your dyke cousin?"

Cora's mouth fell open. "I knew it."

"Oh my gosh." Mocha should have just kept her mouth shut. "Let's get back to your guests."

"No! Mocha! Listen to me!" She gripped her arm and Mocha noticed a few people looking, including her mother. "Listen, I've known you since we were children. I've *seen* you with boys. You know how our family is, and maybe I'm not always as sensitive as I should be, and I'm sorry, but you know that if anybody called you *the dyke cousin* at Christmas I'd punch their teeth out and I wouldn't care if they were my own mom!"

Speaking of, Aunt Elsie was fast approaching, and Cora's voice dropped low. "Mocha. If your own mom and dad disowned you and you had to come live with me and Mason to get away and be who you are, we'd have your back. In a heartbeat. You deserve to be as happy as I feel right now." She glanced back with a small frown at her approaching mom and dropped her voice even lower. "And if that's with another sweet girl then good for you."

And she kissed her on the cheek and very intentionally went to talk to somebody else, ignoring her own mother.

So Aunt Elsie stopped in front of Mocha, the easy target. "I thought we were going to have blue candles mixed in with the pink roses?"

"Mason and Cora decided they would take away from the roses and the candlesticks." She very deliberately brought Mason into it because, sadly, his word seemed to hold more weight with Cora's parents.

"I don't remember discussing candlesticks."

"I know right? Thanksgiving was so long ago, it's so hard to remember everything we discussed! But they came out beautiful! I've already heard so many comments on how lovely the décor choices were."

Aunt Elsie drifted off to talk to somebody else, looking at least somewhat appeased, and Mocha blew a small sigh of relief. Maybe growing up in her family and constantly having to change the subject, sugarcoat, and avert, had made her so well-equipped for this line of work.

And now that she finally had a second to think about what Cora had just said, she couldn't shake it. Maybe having even just one person in her corner was what she needed.

But before she could really ponder how she felt, she witnessed the most uncomfortable world-collide she'd ever experienced in her life. Mom had dragged Dad across the room to meet… Ashley. Mocha put on her fast wedding walk and appeared at their side in record time.

"Mochi! I was just telling your father about the stunning pictures Ashley's taken of everything."

"Well this is just a very good-looking family across the board," Ashley said. "So I've had good models."

"I didn't realize Ashley worked on Bea Lance's wedding too!" Mom turned her attention back to Mocha.

"We worked a couple of weddings together this summer," Mocha said quickly.

"So this is your full-time thing, then?" Dad asked Ashley.

"It is."

"No day job or anything?"

"Dad!" Mocha blurted.

"No, no, I think it's impressive to be in such an artsy field and make a living. What *do* photographers make these days?"

"Dad. Stop." Mocha's face was flooded with embarrassment.

"She doesn't have to tell me what *she* makes!" He protested. "I guess I'm just wondering what the average is. I'm fascinated by gig economy."

Ashley didn't look too unsettled. "I don't really know what the national average is. My numbers are probably a little different."

"You can't do too bad for yourself. You have a very nice house and you don't seem to have a roommate anymore."

Mocha thought about tackling him to shut him up.

Ashley, luckily, didn't look too stricken. "I've been in it for a long time and been in a few magazines and won a few awards and I'm willing to travel. I have a large client base here and in Wisconsin and I shoot multiple weddings a week. So, again, my numbers probably aren't average. It took some time to get my business where I want it, but it's been worth it."

"Wow." He looked at Mocha like he was making some kind of point and Mocha had never before that moment realized what a douche her father could be. "That's a lot of work just to make ends meet."

Ashley raised an eyebrow that said a lot, at least to Mocha. It was a *'Fine, if you want to get tacky and talk money'* look. "It was at first. But last year was my third six-figure year in a row."

Dad's face… was priceless.

"*Really?*"

"Oh yes, weddings are where the money is. Your daughter's in a lucrative line of work."

Mocha had never wanted so badly to high-five Ashley. And hug her. And kiss her. Definitely kiss her.

"Oh, well this is all just a gig for Mocha."

Oh no.

"Is it?" Now Ashley raised an eyebrow in Mocha's direction.

"She's actually going to start interning with Warren & Warren while she works on her MBA."

"Aren't they a finance company?" The little furrow of confusion in Ashley's brow deepened.

"A professional services firm," Mocha answered, vacantly.

"Oh," Mom patted Dad's arm. "Dinner is starting."

Mocha was seated with her parents and felt like a deflated child.

Dinner went by without incident and then

speeches started and Aunt Elsie eagerly grabbed up the microphone. Mocha stole a sip of her mother's cocktail.

"I won't be speaking tomorrow, I'll leave that up to her father because I will be crying much too hard." And she turned on the waterworks right then.

Mocha swigged from her mom's drink again.

"So now is my chance to thank you all for being here. And to talk a little about my daughter Cora."

Here we go, Mocha internally moaned.

"Cora was a very colicky baby. She cried for the first four months of her life." And she went on to describe what a detestable baby Cora had been, and how she and her dear cousin Mochi had burned Mr. Elephant's face off, and what a rebellious teen Cora had been, and how she'd pretty much ruined her parent's life, but, "It's all been worth it. Because now she's the woman sitting before me today."

Cora looked *a little* less annoyed when the speech came to its sweet conclusion, and Mocha felt some relief. A few of the bridal party members who weren't giving speeches at the reception said a few words, and all was sweet and cute and nice until their cousin, Janine, green-eyed monster who couldn't handle any happiness that wasn't her own, somehow got ahold of the microphone.

"Hi everybody. I'm the bride's cousin."

There was a lot of snorting. Half the people in attendance were the bride's cousins. And of course, they all knew what an attention hog Janine was.

Mocha thought that the groom looked a little bit ill.

"Cora. I am really so truly very happy for you." She gave a coy little giggle. "Even though I definitely had him first!"

Oh. My. God.

Across the room, she saw Ashley's mouth fall slightly ajar behind her camera.

And Mocha, glad she had very intentionally seated herself and her parents in a remote corner, waved wildly to the audio-visual guy, who promptly cut the mic off.

"Oh, sorry folks," he came on over the loudspeaker. "Looks like we are having some conveniently timed technical difficulties."

And everybody, thank goodness, laughed at his making light of the uncomfortable speech.

Cora stared blankly at Mason, who drank heavily from his glass.

Mocha caught the AV guy's attention again and pointed to the slideshow screen, and he gave a quick and barely perceptible nod.

"We have, courtesy of the bride and groom's mothers, a little montage of their love story."

People awwwed, as the screen came to life with two pictures of them as children. And luckily, the slideshow was adorable, appropriately cheesy, and uneventful. It concluded with an enchanting photo of them on the porch swing at their engagement party.

The bride and groom gave out gifts to the wedding party and then in a final twist the groomsmen said, "We have a gift for you too, Mason!" He opened it up—and then promptly crammed it back in the bag.

When the guests dwindled Mocha ran after Cora. "How's the bride feeling?" she asked cautiously.

Cora waved her hand in dramatic flair. "We half-finished our wedding weekend bingo card already. I guess it's not a challenge for our loved ones to make idiots of themselves."

Mocha laughed in relief at her good humor. "I'm going to steal your wedding bingo card idea and give it to brides with families as manic as ours."

"And before you ask, Mason told me, *way* back when, that he'd briefly dated someone I was related to before. I just told him that since I'm related to a good quarter of the town population, I wasn't surprised. As long as it wasn't my mom or my sisters I didn't care." She scowled. "I just didn't know it was freaking Jealous Janine. I thought he had better taste."

"Well, he's developed excellent taste because now he's with you. And you say the word and I'll have her removed from the premises at any time."

"I may hold you to that."

Mocha hugged her before they parted, but Cora didn't let her get away just yet. "I saw your parents talking to Ashley," she whispered.

"Cora. We're not here to talk about me."

"I wanna know what happened."

"My dad pried about how much money someone makes in 'the gig economy.'"

"Ew. Not cool."

"The look on his face when she oh-so-casually dropped that she makes six figures… made me hotter for her than I have ever been."

Cora squealed with laughter and delight and Mocha realized she'd just completely admitted wanting Ashley out loud to another human. It hadn't been that hard, either.

"That is the sexiest thing I have ever heard! You could be a trophy wife, Mocha."

"You are the only wife I am worried about. Go to bed."

"Okayyy. I just need to find my groom for a decompression make-out session first."

"Don't get caught," was Mocha's sage advice. Just as they were about to part on the steps of the mansion Mocha doubled back. "Oh! Do I get to know what the groomsmen got Mason?"

"A cock ring. *Highly inappropriate gift* was definitely on the bingo card."

CHAPTER 21

Mocha had found her room earlier before the chaos started, and now she couldn't find it. She wandered down several halls, looking dazedly for any number remotely near *207* and turning up empty.

She turned a corner and saw a door open, and beyond it, mellow light and a whole ton of books. She also thought she caught a glimpse of a wedding dress in there—Cora's wedding dress.

Confused as hell, she stepped inside and saw Ashley, seated on the floor, photographing the lace train of Cora's dress against the backdrop of antique lanterns. Candles and Cora's jewelry glittered on a table in the middle of the room.

Ashley looked up and they looked at each other for a long, unintentional moment.

Ashley gathered her composure first. "Cora asked me to take detail shots in the library. Since the groomsmen are getting ready here in the morning she okayed me to get a head start. Asked for candlelight."

She stood. "And having open flames this close to old books and a wedding dress is the most stressed I have been in a very long time."

Mocha grinned softly. "I'm told I'm quite the pyromaniac, so maybe I can help."

Ashley nodded and Mocha stepped into the room. "Find a spot to dangle the earrings. Maybe from the bindings of a pretty book."

Mocha got to work picking the perfect tome and settled on a giant green one called *The History of Courtly Love*. She dangled the pearl earrings just so from the book, still perched on the shelf, and Ashley captured it.

They passed a good hour like this. She found a book with gorgeous watercolor illustrations that Ashley layered the jewelry across the pages of. They perched the rings in the center of a cover with an ornate border. They hung the dress against the quaint double windows and pushed them open to capture the train billowing in the air.

And when they were about finished they sat in the middle of the floor, trying to get Cora's ring to perch just right on the edge of a lantern to catch the light properly.

"I feel like I've met my details-oriented soulmate," Mocha said simply, finally getting the ring to perch just right. It caught the candle and lamp light beautifully.

Ashley snapped several photos. "I know," she said,

a little sadly. "I get excited just watching you work." Then quickly, she added, "I'm sorry. I shouldn't say things like that. I don't mean to give you mixed signals."

Mocha didn't know what to say next, so she resorted to her default blurting. "I'm thinking of moving out of my parent's."

"Good. Your mom's a smothered sweetheart who's played up your dad's ego and danced in his shadow too long. And that kind of dynamic is insufferable to live with."

It was strange hearing such a simple outside perspective of her parent's relationship, like some complicated mystery she'd been haunted by all her life was just decoded in an instant.

"Sorry he was being such a prick."

"It's fine. There's something so satisfying about winning a dick-measuring contest as a woman."

Mocha laughed in surprise. And Ashley, finished snapping photos, looked up at her. "I'm going to put everything away. You should close the door."

Mocha felt an immediate heat between her legs. "Close the door?"

"I need to talk to you."

Mocha didn't know what to make of that but she got up to close the door while Ashley put everything safely away.

She paused for a long minute, her hand still on the knob, gathering herself. When she turned Ashley was close by.

And her eyes were concerned.

"You're going to work for Warren & Warren?"

She wilted internally. She didn't want to think about any of it.

"I don't know. I was offered the internship but that's not where my heart is. And I don't know how I'd make it work with school and weddings. Of course, my parents want me to give up weddings."

Ashley stepped a little closer. "If you needed a place to go… it would be complicated. Because I do have feelings for you. But if they ever booted you out for being who you are or flipped out because they couldn't control you anymore, you know I'd be here for you. And I have friends near MSU who would be happy to help if you needed somewhere to go."

This support, after Cora's, made her throat tight with tears.

Ashley cupped her chin.

"I am going back to Wisconsin for a while."

Mocha's heart stilled.

"For how long?"

"Most of my September weddings are there. And after… I don't know how much I'll be in town. But if you need me. Just say the word."

Her hand crept up into Mocha's curls. And Mocha resisted kissing her with everything in her.

"I really hoped it would be easier if we cut it off," Ashley whispered, resting her forehead against Mocha's. "But… it still hurts."

"I just want you more," Mocha whispered.

And Ashley kissed her, hand still in her hair. And Mocha kissed tenderly and deeply back.

When Ashley pulled away she whispered, "Tonight I… would… if you wanted."

Mocha only breathlessly nodded.

"Your room?"

"If we can find it."

"Ashley," Mocha gasped, as Ashley collapsed naked against her, kissing her neck and rubbing her clit with one hand. "Oh my God. Ashley…" She arched her back to give Ashley even better access to her vulva, and Ashley eagerly took the offering, caressing her fiercely while she kissed her neck and lips and chest and breasts.

She gasped as Ashley suckled her nipple and tangled her fingers in her hair.

To start, Ashley didn't talk as much as their lovemaking in Saugatuck. But she didn't seem to be any less enraptured.

She guided Mocha into turning onto her stomach and whispered into her ear, "Get on all fours, please. With your bottom facing me. I want to see your pretty little ass."

Oh, God.

She propped up obediently, tremblingly, and felt Ashley squeeze her bottom. Then gasped in surprise when Ashley pried her legs apart.

She began to stroke her wet pussy from this angle, and Mocha groaned in agonized ache.

"You're okay," she whispered gently, gliding a finger in, and then extracting it to rub her clit again, finger covered in wetness this time.

"Ashley," she gasped, the gasp closer to a scream.

"Relax, baby girl," she whispered, stroking more intensely. She dipped her finger inside of Mocha again, and thrust a few times, and then withdrew to stroke her clit again, and she kept the agonizing rhythm up, only increasing in intensity.

Mocha bucked against her hand and she cried out when she came, louder than she meant.

"Oh. My. God."

Ashley startled her by caressing between her legs in the aftermath of her climax, and whispering, "I want so badly to do so many things to you. Things you've never dreamed of."

That only spurred on Mocha's desire. "I want to taste you," she pled.

Ashley lifted her head slightly. "Are you sure?"

"Yes, I want to. I'll kneel on the floor. You get to the edge."

And for once it was Ashley who obeyed, propping herself with her womanhood spread open just at the edge of the bed.

Mocha grabbed a pillow to kneel on, and almost lost her nerve when faced with Ashley in all her loveliness.

"I… won't be as good as you."

"Oh, sweetheart," Ashley's breasts rose with each

ragged breath. "You know that I'm safe for you to explore. I just want you."

Mocha knelt on the pillow and took a deep breath of her and her scent and sight. She slid her tongue slowly at first, but it was enough to make Ashley arch and gasp.

Her legs started trembling.

Drunk on that power, Mocha went on, drawing her tongue all the way up to her clit.

"Ohhh, Mocha." Ashley buried her fists in the blankets.

And Mocha buried her tongue in Ashley, sinking into her sweet folds and savoring deeply.

Feeling Ashley softly grind against her tongue was torturous heaven.

And that's how they were, Mocha deeply savoring the taste of Ashley's intimates and Ashley naked, arching, clinging to the covers…

When the door flew open.

CHAPTER 22

"Oh my God, oh my God, oh my God!"

Mocha grabbed a blanket that had fallen to the edge of the bed and pulled it around herself.

It was her mother standing in the doorway.

"Mom what the *fuck?!*"

Mom was too stunned, too paralyzed to react properly.

She thrust the door closed again.

Ashley had shot up and huddled under the comforter and her mouth hung open in shock.

"Did that just happen?" She turned her intense hazel brown eyes to Mocha. "Did that just fucking happen? Mocha, I am so sorry!"

Mocha only grabbed her sweater and pulled it on as quickly as she could.

"Mocha, do you need me to talk to her?"

"No. I will. I should. Just. Just wait."

She couldn't breathe.

She staggered into the hall where Mom was still standing, dumbstricken, and slammed the door behind her.

"Mom," she could only say, raggedly.

Mom struggled to get out words. "I think they thought we were all staying together and gave me the key to your room." Her voice was stunned and devoid of emotion.

Mocha buried her hands in her hair. "Oh my God. Dad didn't hear or see anything?"

"He's not here," Mom said dazedly. "He's still talking to all your uncles."

Mocha shrank to the hallway floor. "Mom it was… that was… we just…"

"You don't have to explain," she said, blankly. "Not… yet."

"Please don't fucking run to Dad about this."

She'd never used this much language in front of her mother, but Mom didn't wilt away like she'd never been exposed to an f-bomb before.

She opened her mouth—but took a minute to speak. "No, I'd never tell your father. It would break his heart."

Mocha covered her face with her hands. With no small venom, she whispered, "Well I'm sorry that me being a sexual being would ruin his life. I didn't mean to throw away everything you gave me by being a human."

"You know that's not what I mean."

She uncovered her face, stained with tears. "Then what *do you mean?*"

Mom didn't look like she knew what to say.

Finally, she said, "Just. Don't make your cousin's weekend about you."

It felt callous. Like Mom never really known her at all.

Which of course, Mocha realized, she hadn't.

Mom's eyes welled with tears and crying was the most painful thing she could have done. After a lifetime of being the golden daughter, the perfect princess, she'd turned out a disappointment. "And maybe think about how your choices affect everyone else," she said. And she left.

And she was left alone in the hall, a grown woman feeling like a teenager who'd done something abominable.

Ashley, body covered in a hoodie, quietly eased open the door, came into the hall, and sank beside her on the floor.

"I'm so sorry."

Mocha just shook her head. "You were right. It was bound to implode sometime."

Ashley gathered her into her arms.

"She looked at me like she regretted I existed."

Rage flared in Ashley. "I know you are not ready to hear this. But that is not how a loving parent treats their child. And that's on them for being selfish, not you."

Mocha could only bury her head in Ashley's chest and cry.

"Do you think she'll talk to your Dad?"

"No," she whispered. "It's too atrocious in her mind."

Then Ashley knew full well she needed to get out of the picture before it reached anyone else.

"It's my fault. I shouldn't have asked you."

"No." Mocha shook her head, still buried in Ashley's sweater. "I wanted to be with you." Her voice was choked. "I always want to be with you."

Ashley's heart felt like a brick in her chest.

"I love you, Mocha. I know it… wouldn't have worked. But I don't want you to doubt that I really loved you. Very much."

Mocha only cried harder.

Cora's dad gave a cringe little speech about purity at the altar. "Mason, I've always known I could trust you to protect and honor my daughter. And Cora, I've always known you were in good hands."

Literally, Mocha thought to herself. She could *feel* the smug smile oozing off of Cora but her own hands were balled into tight fists. What a grotesque little world of trying to control everyone and everything.

She was finished with it.

When Mocha had woken up this morning Ashley had still been in bed with her, an arm protectively around her, the other hand stroking her hair. *"Are you okay?"* she'd asked quietly.

"Just… humiliated."

And Ashley had kissed the back of her neck and she was now tuning out her uncle's droning words at the altar, remembering it…

A row ahead of her, she noticed a commotion. Janine was furiously fanning herself and swaying ever-so-slightly in her seat. Her parents leaned in to ask if their little princess was okay and she waved that she was.

Then not a minute later—she fainted.

There were a few hushed gasps that she hoped no one at the altar could hear, and she lunged to the next row.

"Give her room," Mocha whispered, squeezing past her aunt, uncle, and Janine's younger brother, and waving them away. "Janine?" She fanned her face with a program and stealthily waved one of their nearby cousins over.

"Janine, I'm going to have Daniel carry you outside and we'll get you home." She said it deadpan.

And sure enough, Janine's eyes flew open. "No! No, I want to see our cousin happily married."

"You are *so* sweet and selfless Janine, but your health isn't worth it. We're getting you home."

"No!" She hissed it a little loudly and sat up a little too quickly. "I'm great. I'm fine. Thank you, Mocha. You're the sweetest."

And luckily, the bride and the groom, who were in the middle of their sand ceremony, seemed none the wiser.

Mocha sat back down and puffed out a heated sigh. She was seated on the edge of the pew, with Dad wedged firmly between herself and Mom.

The rest of the wedding ceremony passed without incident.

During their receiving line, Janine made eyes at Mason and hugged him long while whispering, "I am *so* happy for you. Really. You picked the right one."

Mocha distracted Cora with a longer hug until Janine finally walked away.

"Did you just straightjacket-hug me?"

"No, what are you talking about?" Mocha laughed. "It was so beautiful Cora. You're stunning."

And Mocha hoped to high heaven that was the end of Janine's antics, but she wouldn't be so lucky. She hurried to the reception hall to make sure everything was in place before folks started drifting over.

She noticed Ashley photographing the empty hall and the centerpieces. All night long Ashley had held her, comforting her. Mocha couldn't shake the sickening feeling that she'd held her like she was saying goodbye.

Mocha knew she had to stay in the wedding zone, that she was in the home stretch, but last night haunted her in more ways than one.

She jumped into the kitchen, where things seemed to be abuzz and ready to go, and then went to check on the cake.

Janine was there, hovering precariously close to the cake table, and she was carrying a paper bag. It looked like she fully intended to pour whatever was in that bag onto the cake.

Mocha froze.

"What the hell are you doing?"

Janine jumped, and when she saw who it was, her eyes widened.

"Just finding a quiet place to rest."

"What is that?"

"A puke bag."

"Then *why* do you have it so close to the cake?"

"I haven't puked in it yet!"

Ashley approached them. "Someone was wanting to know where the favor table was supposed to be wheeled to?" She looked in confusion at the two tense women. "Everything okay?"

"Why don't you tell me what's in that bag, Janine?"

"Because it's nothing. Okay? And I'm going."

"Janine. If you don't show me what you were going to put on that cake table—"

Janine made a beeline for the door.

Ashley blocked her exit and Mocha seized the bag and looked inside. She let out a small cry of horror and dropped it.

"You backwoods piece of *shit!*"

Ashley looked like she'd have normally laughed if she wasn't absolutely shocked.

"Janine," Mocha had hit her limit. She straightened. "I am going to call the police if you don't leave."

"It's just a wedding prank!"

"No! A wedding prank is condom balloons on the groom's car, Janine! *This* is a health code violation, it's cruel, it's desperate, and I'm sorry, but allowing somebody else *five seconds of happiness* will not ruin your shallow, miserable little life!"

Tears welled in Janine's eyes because she was *clearly* the victim here. She released a sob and ran towards the door and this time Ashley stepped aside to let her leave.

Mocha covered her face.

"It's a dead mouse Ashley, *it's a fucking dead mouse!*"

"Are you serious?"

"I'm going to vomit, I can't even touch the bag."

"It's okay. I got it." And Ashley stooped to quickly pluck up the bag.

"As much as it makes me want to gag we should take photos first. In case she tries to come back and we need evidence later. I don't think the moron knew there were cameras in here too, so she'd be fucked."

"It's okay. I'll take the photos somewhere else. And I've got it."

"Thank you." Mocha was sick of rage-crying and reigned it in.

"I would hug you but I'm going to deal with this quick." Ashley pinched the bag carefully. "You're okay. You're amazing."

"Thank you, Ashley." She rubbed her forehead. "Thank you so much."

Okay. Make it through this day. Make it through this day. Then she figured out how to extricate herself from… all of this.

"Mocha, what is going on?" Dad found her in the reception hall, Mom shuffling silently in tow. "Dan and Sarah are furious. Janine came to them crying saying you were threatening to have her thrown out by the police?"

"Yes." Mocha looked each of them in their faces, so completely thoroughly done with sugarcoating. "I caught her trying to put a dead rodent on the cake table. If she tries to come back in here I definitely will call the police. And you can tell Dan and Sarah I said exactly that."

And she marched on, reveling in the shocked looks on their faces.

Without Janine, the evening was a magic one. Cora was aglow, Mason was all over her, and they were happy. Aunt Elsie was in too much of a mother of the bride flurry to notice the color changes, and Cora wore her glow-in-the-dark Vans with her bustled dress, and when the lights fell glowsticks lit up the dance floor. And not a single person's life was ruined.

"One last totally epic wedding for the summer season." Ashley sighed, appearing at her side. But at that second one of her aunts appeared to ask when they should hand out the exit wands and Mocha was pulled away.

Before the exit, Cora hugged her tight. "Gosh,

what a great day!"

"You are stunning. It's all been so stunning."

"Thanks to you." Cora pulled away, grinning from ear to ear. "And throwing Janine out was the best gift you could've given us. 'Tear the whole family apart' was on our bingo card, and I think this will just about do it!"

The exit was just as magical as if there had been real sparklers, with all the glitter and glow.

Mocha went to find Ashley then—but she was nowhere to be found. Her Mom wasn't anywhere to be found either. Just Dad, and he tugged her aside to say, "What a good day Mocha. I'm sure your turn will come soon."

CHAPTER 23

She woke up, after a good nine hours of sleep, to a text.

I've loved every second of this summer with you. This was the last wedding I committed to in Michigan until later in the fall, and most of the weddings I have left this year are closer to Wisconsin than Harper Port, so I'll be gone for a while. I'm excited for all the contracts I have lined up with you next year.

Next year?

A second text.

But I meant everything I said. If you need help or to get out, just call.

And a third text.

I wanted to thank you. With you, I've learned to forgive myself for wanting to heal and move on. I hope with all my heart you find freedom for yourself and don't let go of the work that you love. You are incredibly good at creating beauty.

―――∞―――

All the fire Mocha had found at the wedding vanished.

She could find no point in rupturing her whole life if she didn't know Ashley would be on the other side.

Ashley turned her house into an Airbnb while she was away, and not a few days after she left guests started sifting in and out. Dad looked enraged at the *California* and *Oregon* license plates.

Ashley had hired a service to maintain the house and never surfaced herself between visitors.

Seeing it devoid of her made the image of the glass dollhouse feel hollow. Ashley, of course, had never been a doll who was trapped in it. She was real and she was gone and she was somewhere out there living a life.

Mocha managed to avoid Mom and Warren & Warren for a couple of days. And then one early morning she stepped off the porch cradling a tote of binders and notebooks more limply than usual, and Mom was there, reading and drinking orange juice on the front porch.

She hadn't seen her mother look contemplative in so long that she had to do a double-take.

Mom looked almost embarrassed to be caught away from the stove or her vacuum cleaner. "I guess we need to talk."

She stayed back, like a wary deer. "Is there anything to talk about?"

Dad's car was gone, so they were alone. Her mother patted the chair beside her and Mocha stiffly took it.

They were silent a long minute and Mocha stared out on the lawn. She normally looked forward to autumn and the start of a new semester, but now it all just sounded overwhelming and cold and kind of empty.

Mom cleared her throat. "I just didn't know what to say. That night. All I ever wanted was for you to have a good husband and a family and this was all really hard to accept."

"Well. She's gone and it's over. So. I guess you won't have to accept it."

Mother wrung her hands and cleared her throat again. "Ashley was a good person."

"She was an incredible person."

"She talked to me before she left."

Mocha finally looked directly at her mother. Mom, however, didn't meet her eyes, clinging frailly to her cup of OJ, keeping her gaze trained on the flower baskets.

"After the wedding, when you were busy wrapping everything up." She faltered a good long while again.

"What did she say?" Mocha asked, breathless.

"She only begged me to love and support you. To be there for you. And it struck me... how ironic and..." she swallowed. "Sad it was, that she was asking me, your parent, just to love and accept you."

Mocha kept her hands firmly clamped on each arm of the wicker chair like it might support her.

"I'm so sorry, Mocha. I was raised to believe that for a woman to be with another woman was a selfish choice. That it was somehow robbing a good man of a chance to have a wife. That it robbed your parents of the chance to be grandparents, robbed you of a normal family and children."

She sat up straighter. "But. Really *selfish* was trying to control you. And selfish was being jealous of my own daughter for having the freedom to make her own choices. And selfish was thinking that my daughter was somehow robbing the world by choosing her own happiness."

Mocha didn't know what to say.

"I'm sorry," Mom repeated.

And Mocha numbly nodded, unable to quite believe this was happening, unable to quite trust that it was.

When she could form words all she could say was, "I love you, Mom. And I need to go for a drive."

Mom nodded. And for once in her life, she didn't ask her where she was going.

She didn't have a destination in mind either.

She drove aimlessly through town and a few of the empty roads surrounding. When she drove back into town she passed through what people called The Old Historic neighborhood. Cosmos were growing absolutely everywhere, probably the last of the summer. She slowed a little to admire them.

The purples were her favorite. So wildflower-looking and hardy, bouncing in the faint breeze in the middle of all that green. Pinpricks of cosmic colorful wonder, always.

She slammed the brakes. This was stupid.

She had to break free for her own sake. She didn't know if Ashley's heart could take any more, if she would be there, in a life where she was free. But God, she hoped she would be. Because she was worth everything.

She drove, with a lot more direction, to the Flower Box.

She ordered a giant tea and her plan was to sit and scroll furiously through her tablet and scribble in her notebook like she always did to sort things out. New price points, new possibilities, updating her website, looking at listings near MSU, looking at her student account, looking at options, carving out freedom, and maybe even rethinking her MBA dream.

But while she was still in line, somebody tapped her shoulder.

"You were Bea Lance's wedding planner, weren't you?" The woman had a southern accent.

"That was me." She smiled slightly.

"My little girl was just in love with that whole wedding and I was gonna get in touch ASAP. I wanna know what I have to do to lock you in!"

Mocha got her tea and followed the woman to a tall table and chairs.

"Well, I do normally have to talk to the couple, I need at least one of them present before I commit to anything."

"Of *course!* My daughter's at the boutique next door, I'm texting her to run over right now."

"Does she have dates in mind?" Mocha asked, lowering her bag.

"Honey, we'll pick any date you are free. We need all the help we can get. She wants a summer or fall wedding and I want to keep my head on straight."

For all her frazzle, the woman had a warm presence and Mocha relaxed a little. Not a second later the bride appeared, scurrying through the morning light towards the Flower Box. She was an adorable younger version of her mother, and greeted Mocha with an exuberant hug, like they'd always known each other. "Bea's wedding was just so beautiful, and she said you kept her so calm and just took all the panic out of everything, and we need that. So bad we need that. We're a lot of fun but we are just a mess!"

She plopped down.

As they started chatting, the girl lapsed into dreamy reveries about her southern-whimsical vision and how all she knew was that it had to feel southern, it had to be whimsical, sunflowers had to be incorporated, and she had to have at least one shade of blue.

Mocha scribbled in a notebook and then finally showed them both the figure she'd jotted there. "I'd love to work with you—" she almost started off by apologizing for her prices but refrained. "And you can take all the time you need to think about the investment, especially since you don't have a date locked in. But this would be my rate and this would be my deposit."

It was more than four times the pittance she'd been charging all summer.

And there was not a second's pause.

Mom whipped out her checkbook. "We'll pay twice the deposit right now just to lock you in and get a head start on paying this puppy off."

Half her pay-in-full price.

"Well that was easy," Mocha laughed, and so did the bride-to-be. "I'll get the digital contract up for you to sign!"

And in a matter of minutes, it was done.

She hugged them both. "I can't wait to work with you. Your wedding is going to be so beautiful."

And that was that.

Mocha sat for a long minute staring at the check.

With this and everything she'd saved this summer, she'd be good for at least several month's rent and living expenses. She had her life's savings that she could look at when it came to at least first semester's tuition. And she still had weddings to work this fall...

She took a deep breath.

Hope pulsed in her veins. A future with no hope of Ashley was too much to think of and she could only hope her parents would feel the same way about her.

She gave Warren & Warren a phone call.

When she got home Dad was on a tirade. She sorted through their incoming mail as a distraction.

"I bumped into Clark and his wife at the store. He told me their daughter and son-in-law have *elected* not to have children. *Elected.*"

Mom looked like she didn't know what expression to put on her face while she mixed the dry ingredients for whatever it was she was baking.

Dad went on. "I just thought they were trying to be all modern, traveling and not having a family right away while Laura's eggs wilted away. Why do kids even get married these days if they have no interest in starting a family?"

Mocha fought so hard not to roll her eyes that she had to physically rub them to stop them. "Some people love each other Dad."

"Hmm?"

She spoke up louder. "Some people get married because they *love each other* and want to be a family, Dad. A family can have two people."

He snorted a laugh. "Yes. Romantic. Having no one to take care of you when you're old."

She flipped slowly and deliberately through her mail. "Is that why you had me?"

"Hmm?"

"Is that why you had me? Just so you have someone to take care of you when you're old?"

He clearly wasn't catching on to how serious she was. He laughed. *"Yes,* Mocha," he said sarcastically. "And to run out and make us millions." He turned back to Mom. "It's probably for the best. Their son-in-law turned down a prestigious partnership to work in environmental law instead. Maybe Laura doesn't *want* to have kids with him."

He sat at the table where Mom was furiously folding in the flour.

"And of course you heard about Stephen and Steve. I saw Steve's poor dad at the bank—"

Mocha dropped her bag loudly on the hardwood floor.

"Now is probably a good time to tell you that I just turned down Warren & Warren. And that I'm not popping out grandkids just so you can have them as a consolation prize for raising me. And that I'm in love with another woman."

CHAPTER 24

She wasn't stopping.

"And your-house-your-rules is too heavy a price to pay just to be financially hostage to you. So I'm moving out. And this 'party planning gig' is what I do. I'm building a business and a career doing it. And I'm sorry. I'm an adult. And I'm not your perfect little princess. And I'm sorry that I'm not sorry. And in case you're wondering, it's our next-door neighbor that I love. It's Ashley Montez. Blake Kelvin can take his football play stories to hell for all I care."

Dad looked like she'd thrown a brick at his head.

And Mom looked teary-eyed, but not in the same way she'd looked at Cora's wedding.

She looked almost proud.

And someday, they'd all talk about this, but she'd

let them talk over her for all her life and today was not the day.

"And I'm taking a trip to Wisconsin. I don't know when I'll get back. I'll move out when I do."

She didn't know where she'd move out to. Maybe Cora's vacated apartment. Maybe... She flushed to think of sharing more with Ashley, maybe a life and home together.

She didn't know.

But it was time to go.

She went upstairs to cram some things into her weekend bag, her tote of notebooks conveniently ready to go.

When she got back downstairs Dad was nowhere to be seen, but Mom was waiting for her by the door.

She hugged her. Just hugged her. It was a start.

She pulled into a gas station in Deerfield Illinois to text Ashley an hour before she crossed the border.

She'd blitzed through Indiana, Illinois, and would hit Wisconsin shortly, all in one afternoon. After 2.5 decades of never leaving Michigan, four states in one day wasn't half bad.

She had no plan, didn't know whether Ashley was even in Madison right now, and didn't even know if Ashley would see her, but she had to try.

What are you doing today? She tapped out.

And then she pressed send. She stopped again just before crossing the border and saw Ashley's reply. *Heading to the North Point Lighthouse. I'll send pictures.*

For a photoshoot?

Ashley responded right away. *Just for me.*

Mocha quickly plugged in the distance. 43 minutes from here.

Will you still be there in like 45 minutes?

Probably. And then another message. *Um, why?*

No reason. Just make sure you are.

And Mocha pressed on, heart beating out of her chest.

Her GPS app boomed, "Welcome to Wisconsin!" with minimal enthusiasm.

How had she never been out of her home state?

Wisconsin was green with endless trees and bodies of water visible from the highway. And what her little Michigander heart would never allow herself to admit, even to herself, was how eerily similar to Michigan and like-home it felt. Just like Michigan, the nothingness was quaintly, endearingly boring.

Her anxiety mounted when she crossed over into Milwaukee, closer to the lighthouse, and closer to Ashley.

The street she pulled onto was lined with trees and quaint houses, but no lighthouse that she could see. She almost forgot to put the vehicle in park and then almost tried to climb out of the car without unbuckling her seatbelt.

She followed a path that ran alongside the trees and eventually broke through them, revealing a whitewashed building with red roofing, and then finally, the trees cleared enough to reveal a lighthouse attached. She scanned the grounds for Ashley but didn't see her. The land was sprawling, with grass and bridges and more trees and what looked like trails.

The grass-lined path she was on ran to the lighthouse and she followed it. Seeing it in the real world, ripped right out of the photos on Ashley's wall, felt a little like seeing Ashley in real life for the first time. Jarring, but not off-putting. Somehow more enchanting than the static visual.

When she reached the lighthouse she kept walking past it, seeing people further ahead walking dogs and leading around children.

Finally, she spotted Ashley, standing by a bridge, dark hair whipped by the breeze. The bridge was guarded by lion statues and Ashley was leaning beside one, flicking through pictures on her camera, leaving Mocha free to approach her without being seen.

When she got into Ashley's line of sight Ashley did a double-take.

She looked stricken.

"Mocha?" She lowered her camera back into its bag, not looking away from Mocha's approach. "What the hell are you doing here?"

"Begging you to take me."

She threw her arms around Ashley and she kissed her deeply. But she could feel the faint resistance, the confusion, the fear of hoping.

She released her. "I told my father he could fuck himself this morning. Or, roughly the equivalent." She took both her hands, which Ashley returned limply. "Told him I was moving out. That I turned down Warren & Warren today. And that I was in love with another woman. That I was in love with you."

Ashley stared at her, her eyes not daring to hope. "You didn't."

"I did. Named you by name and everything."

Ashley didn't look quite sure whether to believe it or not.

Mocha finally registered the view from where they were standing, the water just visible through the trees in one direction, the lighthouse rising in the other.

She tried to lighten the anxiety in the air. "This is really, truly stunning, Ashley."

"You are stunning." And Ashley finally gripped her hands back and tugged her a little bit closer. "Mocha what are you going to do? What about housing? School?"

Mocha tightened her grasp around Ashley's hands, hopefully. "I just booked my first wedding for big-girl prices. She paid me upfront today more than I'm making for my next two weddings combined, and it was only half my rate. I'll figure out housing. I don't know about school. But I'll figure it out like everyone else does."

She couldn't get over Ashley's bewitching eyes and tucked an imploring hand beneath her chin. "And Mom is in my corner. I can't thank you enough for trying to get through to her. So who knows? Maybe I won't be cut off forever like some Jane Austen gentleman."

A glimmer of hope finally lit in Ashley's eyes. "So you're free?"

"Freer than I've been my whole life."

"And… I didn't ruin your whole life? You won't feel like you threw it all away just to be with me?"

"Ashley, what I was doing before you was *hardly* living."

Ashley laughed. And she blinked rapidly like she was blinking away the start of tears. She reached to take the hand Mocha had tucked under her chin, to fasten it against her face.

"Well then. Mocha May Johnson. If you're free, I'd like to take you to dinner. And if you're free tomorrow I'd like to show you my hometown. And if I may be so bold, I'd like to bring you home to my family." She stepped closer. "And if I'll get to see you, I'll be in Michigan a lot more than I was planning to this fall."

"Oh Ash, I'd love it all. And I love you."

"Good." Ashley smiled past a blur of tears, and Mocha thought it was the first time she saw her smile unfettered by any fear. "Because I love you."

And she drew Mocha into a tender kiss.

Before they left the lighthouse Ashley whisked her

around the landmark, gripping her hand tight. She paused to capture a handful of photos of Mocha on the lion bridge and looking up at the lighthouse and tried for a selfie attempt of them both.

"It's a museum. And we can go up in the lighthouse."

The lighthouse staircase spiraled upwards and the snatches of blue water through the window and the trees were vivid. Standing here above the world, overlooking lake Michigan, felt like standing on the verge of everything.

Ashley snapped a photo of Mocha on the brink of it all.

ABOUT THE AUTHOR

Maya Bordeaux escaped a cult. No joke. Luckily, once she escaped into the world that she was raised to hate and fear, she found endless beauty, profound love, and simple acceptance.

These days Maya is proud of everything she was taught to be ashamed of— her bisexuality, her mixed-race heritage, her insatiably curious nature, and her existence as a woman.

Maya lives for all things cozy. Her interests are as diverse as her stories and she has worked at a zoo, a ranch, been a teacher, a librarian, and a small-town journalist. She lives in the middle of nowhere with her love, her blonde dog, and her notebooks.

Made in the USA
Coppell, TX
27 December 2022